OSAMA
VAN
HALEN

**MICHAEL
MUHAMMAD
KNIGHT**

SOFT SKULL PRESS
BROOKLYN

Library of Congress Cataloging-in-Publication Data is available upon request.

ISBN: 978-1-59376-242-1

Cover design by Goodloe Byron
Interior design by Maria E. Torres, Neuwirth & Associates
Printed in the United States of America

Soft Skull Press
An Imprint of Counterpoint LLC
2117 Fourth Street
Suite D
Berkeley, CA 94710

www.softskull.com
www.counterpointpress.com

Distributed by Publishers Group West

10 9 8 7 6 5 4 3 2 1

CONTENTS

OSAMA VAN HALEN

PROGRESSIVE ISLAM

THE DOUBLE-DONG BROTHERS

IT WAS FRIDAY morning and the author was thirsty, but Amazing Ayyub's friends had drunk all his soda. The author went around the house collecting half-empty cans left on tables and windowsills and the TV and poured them into a cup, the last can yielding a cockroach riding Vanilla Coke like it was a waterslide at Darien Lake.

His bedroom had a door going straight to the back porch, cluttered with old pipes, a toilet bowl, and a Little Tikes oven. He walked to the abandoned car in the backyard with one of its windows replaced by a sheet of clear plastic. "How the shit does he sleep in there?" the author muttered as he swung back his boot to kick the driver's-side door. Inside, the skinny skid-row Shiite Amazing Ayyub jumped up with his fist cocked for a cop or robber or whoever and saw that it was only Michael Muhammad Knight.

Ayyub moaned as he crawled out, wearing a gray hooded sweatshirt that said Old Navy and black sweatpants that said G-Unit. Because he acquired his wardrobe by stealing and scavenging around the college campus, there was always something hodge-podge about his clothes. Amazing Ayyub had long ago forgotten that brand names were like philosophical statements, so you'd see him in mismatched rhetoric, like someone's Old Navy hoodie with someone else's G-Unit sweatpants, and he was too genuinely punk to care.

"How was work?" asked the author.

"It was great, bro. I mastered those piss pots."

Michael Muhammad Knight brought Amazing Ayyub inside and said that he should get a key to the house. Ayyub kicked off his rancid boots and slumped into the living room couch, which had been left there by the evictees who had come before Michael and Ayyub. With his spine all bent and his face buried in the cushion, Ayyub took stock of the moment and busted out a shrill whimper of Good Charlotte's "Lifestyles of the Rich and Famous." Good Charlotte was only a glossy caricature of punks like Ayyub, and Ayyub sang the song only to be funny, but he gave it an accidental truth: Here was the real street, the real gutter kid whose ribs really stuck out, saluting the fake MTV translation of himself.

Michael Muhammad Knight sat at the dining room table and stared at the tall, unbound white Hammermill stack of his story, title page on top, with a clean black Times New Roman proclamation in 28-point font: "MUHAMMAD ENTERING FROM THE REAR." Below, in 22: "A NOVEL." Below that, in 16: "BY MICHAEL MUHAMMAD KNIGHT." His story looked strong and heavy, like a hard white brick rather than 842 slivers of paper, twice as thick as normal because his agent wanted it double-spaced.

It was supposed to be a fresh copy with revisions, but he'd be sending her essentially the same manuscript he had a month ago. She had wanted the Arabic stuff taken out.

"Like when they say, 'Insha'Allah,'" she'd explained on the phone. "I don't know what that means."

"It means 'If God wills.'"

"Well, can't they just say, 'If God wills'?"

"No, they can't."

"Why not?"

"I don't know. But they wouldn't say that. And for me to write them as saying that absolutely destroys my credibility. It's like spelling 'Qur'an' with a *K*."

She'd pretended to know what that meant and said she'd get back to him.

There was no reason for his story to be published by anyone remotely mainstream, Arabic lingo or not. Islam and sodomy—what kind of market was that?

He had tried putting the book out himself by printing copies at Kinko's and handing them out for free. He'd gone to a mosque with five copies and seen what he could do.

He couldn't do much. Then he'd started leaving posts on Internet message boards: "If you want a free novel, send me a mailing address, and it's yours."

The Internet posting did find some readers, and he went broke shipping books all over the United States and to six or seven other countries. He included his email address on the inside cover so readers could send him their feedback. They usually did.

"Your novel *Muhammad Entering from the Rear* is misinformed," one declared. "Islam very clearly prohibits sodomy. Rasullullah Muhammad sallallaho alayhe wa salam said, 'Allah does not look at one who comes to his wife in her anus.'"

"I don't get it," said another fan letter. "The book just leads up to a guy doing his girlfriend in the butt. That's your whole story; it all revolves around one act of anal sex." This guy had the author questioning his heightened sense of self-importance. In a beat-up paperback that Michael Muhammad Knight had carried around the Georgetown campus for a week, Albert Camus told him that at some point, every true revolutionary is caused to doubt his revolution. Michael Muhammad Knight wasn't even sure if he had a revolution to doubt. "You're not controversial," said the reader. "You're an idiot."

The hero of *Muhammad Entering from the Rear* was one of those guys who craved a hymen for his trophy wall, but then he fell in love with a girl who had been with one guy before him. He had missed the flower by less than six months and didn't know what to do about it, until he realized that she still had one undiscovered hole—so he took that and settled for the *psychological* hymen of anal virginity.

Michael Muhammad Knight's agent wanted him to rewrite the story as an autobiography, since nobody read novels anymore. He could have done it easily enough—there was a real girl behind that story, and he really had pumped her ass—but she probably wouldn't have wanted to be named for something like that. So he'd kept it as fiction, with the disclaimer that any similarities to actual persons or events, living or dead, were purely coincidental.

A famous punk record label had picked up the do-it-yourself novel for its online catalog. They'd split sales down the middle, and Michael Muhammad Knight had almost broken even, but he still had to make the copies himself, printing them at Kinko's and binding them on the living room floor. To eat, he worked as an overnight janitor in group homes. Amazing Ayyub worked as an overnight janitor at Wal-Mart.

Michael Muhammad Knight's living room smelled of trimethylamine, the chemical that makes decomposing semen reek like rotting garbage. Credit went to Amazing Ayyub.

Noted professors in the fields of Islamic studies and comparative literature began mentioning Michael Muhammad Knight to their classes. His novel found its way into the hands of the world's foremost anarchist thinker, who happened to have spent years in Iran, studying Sufism and opium. The anarchist had a hand in a publishing collective that put out his own books, and he enjoyed *Muhammad Entering from the Rear* so much that Michael Muhammad Knight would no longer have to make it himself.

The publishing collective didn't pay anything, so the agent was fucked, but it did provide authors with complimentary copies of their books, so Michael Muhammad Knight had fifty perfect-bound editions of the new *Muhammad Entering from the Rear*. When the box first arrived, he spent a lot of time caressing the smooth covers. Then he knocked all the terrible books off his shelves and replaced them with his own. The stacks looked artful, all with the same title and the author's name lined up perfectly, one atop the other in columns. The back covers had bar codes on them. Now the do-it-yourself Kinko's author was a published novelist and could worm his way into anthologies. The Islamic Society of North America even invited him to speak at its annual convention. Then a whole new organization, the Progressive Muslim Union, put him on its board of directors.

"What's a Progressive Muslim?" Ayyub asked.

"I don't know."

"Don't cheese out, bro—that sounds like some cheesedick nonsense." When it came to sects and offshoots, Progressive Muslims weren't as cool as Five Percenters. Five Percenters had cool names like Supreme Zig-Zag-Zig Allah; Progressive Muslims had names like Daisy Khan.

With autumn came the Mahdi's birthday. Michael Muhammad Knight wasn't sure how he'd celebrate it, until

Amazing Ayyub came in with his arms full of brightly colored party packs of illegal fireworks.

"*Pennsylvania!*" Ayyub yelled, before the author could ask the question. "It's a special night, bro. Check this out— we've got Roman candles, bottle rockets, M-80s, smoke bombs. We could go down Best Street and take out the armory." Amazing Ayyub emptied his party packs onto the living room floor and spent over an hour merging Green Chrysanthemums, Tiger Tails, Colorful Bees, Dahlia Shells, Red Palm Trees, Floating Leaves, Golden Waves, Silver Crowns, Crackling Rains, and Moving Stars into one giant duct-tape ball with a sophisticated network of intersecting fuses, so that if one firework were lit, they'd all go off. It was enough gunpowder that the smell alone could give someone a headache. At first Ayyub wanted to light it in the backyard, but Michael Muhammad Knight almost slapped him. They drove down to the strip of decay on Tonawanda Street and went behind a closed-down factory. Michael Muhammad Knight kept the car running but turned off the headlights.

"What are we gonna fuckin' say when we're two Muslims getting caught behind a building with duct-taped explosives? 'It's okay, officers, we're honoring Imam Mahdi's birthday— you know, that guy they're crying for in Iraq right now?'"

"Don't you worry about a thing, Michael. I'd fuckin' go to Niagara Falls and cross the border with it strapped to my chest if I wanted to."

"Okay, Ayyub," the author barked, "run over by the fence there, light it, jet back here, and we'll dip out as it pops."

"I'm on the job, bro." Then Amazing Ayyub ran off with the firework bomb, set it down by the fence, and tried getting the lighter to work with his face just inches above the fuses. Once he finally got the thing going, he stood and looked at it for a split second, then ran back to the car. Michael Muhammad Knight hit the gas before Ayyub even had both feet inside. The fireworks whistled and screamed. The author looked in his rearview mirror to see a growing tower of smoke and multicolored fire. He slammed on the brakes just before hitting the street.

"Go put out the fire."

"*Jesus!*" Ayyub hollered. He ran over to the bomb and kicked out the flames, then sprinted back, and they drove away.

"You smell like smoke," said Michael Muhammad Knight.

"The shit was wrapped too tight. The duct tape kept them all from shooting off, so they just burned each other."

"Look at the smoke." They were a block away by that point, but they could still see it looming above the buildings.

"Happy Birthday, ya Qa'im."

"How old is he?" asked the author.

"He was five when Allah put him in ghaybat in 939."

They drove around for at least an hour after that, rolling through previously unknown neighborhoods and getting a far ways from the smoke. Amazing Ayyub noted that they had arrived at a nice section of Delaware Avenue. "Fuck these guys," he said.

"The Mahdi's not driving an SUV," said Michael Muhammad Knight, who imagined the Imam of the Age as a character like the hand-drawn punk heroes seen in thousands of black-and-white photocopied flyers for shows. He'd have spiked hair and a spiked jacket, as the traditions insisted, broad shoulders under black leather, and his back reading Spirit of '77. His fists would be clenched, his knuckles torn up. His green-laced Doc Martens would look to weigh five hundred pounds apiece, planted firmly in the pavement, and he'd stand more like a monument than like a man.

Then they drove down Elmwood Avenue and passed the bowling alley where, Ayyub said, someone had been stabbed in the face. It was either someone or someone's girlfriend; he couldn't remember. Amazing Ayyub liked to roll the window down halfway while keeping the heat on full blast. The author had no clue why he did that—maybe it had something to do with cold Buffalo and sleeping in abandoned cars. Leave that one for the scholars.

They made it to the liquor store on Grant, the one with the white wooden horse in front that Ayyub used to call Zul-Jannah, after the White Horse of Karbala. And from there they went home to their back porch with the toilet bowl and Little Tikes oven. Amazing Ayyub sang some Swingin' Utters lyric that corresponded to the moment—"Sit on the stoop and let the liquid soothe your pride before you go inside"—and Michael Muhammad Knight looked across the backyard to the trampled fence and abandoned car and old, unpainted doghouse. They'd never had a dog; it was just another legacy from the people who used to live there—whose dog must have been a big dog, the author assumed, based on the size of the door.

The next day he and Ayyub went to the Walden Galleria, which had a whole store of just Halloween stuff. It was too crowded to really check out, but he managed to dabble briefly in frotteurism (302.89 in the *Diagnostic and Statistical Manual of Mental Disorders, Vol. 4*): Squirming to make his way through all the people at the front entrance, passing a nice-smelling teenager in low-riding jeans, he turned—and for almost a full second they stood belly to back, his body behind her body, snuggled in close, through no fault of either of them. He didn't do anything inappropriate, but he had an inappropriate head and she knew. He knew she knew.

Ayyub set off a few spare bottle rockets in the mall parking lot. They sat on the back of the author's car for a while, watching girls entering and exiting the food court. At one point the author turned away from Ayyub and watched cars headed for I-90. He turned back around, and Ayyub had on a bright orange Nautica fleece.

"Where the hell'd you get that?"

"I found it."

"Where'd you find it?"

"I don't know. In that car over there."

"I suppose we should get out of here, then."

"Yeah, bro. Hey, you need safety pins?"

"What?"

"I've got safety pins. You want 'em?"

The author put his hand in his pocket and touched his bare leg. "As a matter of fact, I do."

Ayyub dug them out of a pocket on his new fleece. Michael Muhammad Knight pulled his pocket inside out to fix it.

"Was that your beat-off pocket?" Ayyub asked.

"Yes, Ayyub."

"I had one of those, too, one time." It took three or four safety pins for Michael Muhammad Knight to have an intact pocket again. Amazing Ayyub had one left and flicked it at a nearby car. "Brand new cocksucking Volkswagen," he screeched, as a family of five walked past.

"Fantastic, Ayyub."

"THESE PEOPLE NEED TO FUCKING DIE!" Ayyub went over to where the safety pin had landed and positioned it under the VW's tire. "Beautiful Volkswagen," he said. "Beautiful day in upstate New York. This fucker's in for a treat." The author wanted to tell him that the Fifth and Sixth Imams both opposed armed rebellion, but whatever.

Ayyub had bought a pair of dirty dice, with the idea that it'd convince the author to have a party. The dice were big and soft and red and attached by a red string. One had body parts (lips, breasts, neck, "below waist"), and the other had actions (massage, lick, suck). Ayyub said that dirty dice got the ball rolling. Two nights later, the living room where he used to jerk off all the time was filled with high school kids flipping through his porn mags and leaving the Shi'a books alone. Ayyub, a blond slam-pig, and some football player–looking boys were playing cards at the dining room table, Ayyub with his shirt off to show the big Karbala tattoo across his chest. Michael Muhammad Knight sat on the couch between a pretty strawberry blond and a tall, kind of tough brunette who had the dice in her lap.

"Do you know how many shots I've had?" she asked.

"I don't care," said Michael Muhammad Knight. She rolled the dice on the floor.

"Massage neck." The author put his hands on her traps, squeezed, and rubbed for a few seconds, then took the dice.

"Kiss lips." They shared a quick peck, and the strawberry blond took the dice.

"Massage breasts." He looked her in the eye to see if it was cool, shrugged, and went for it. She gave a sarcastic moan and laughed.

The brunette's turn.

"Kiss below waist." She leaned back, and the author kissed her denim crotch. Then he rolled.

"Kiss lips." She had nasty cigarette breath but they kept going, with tongues and tit mauling, and then he heard the strawberry blond say, "Me too" before joining in with sweet Bacardi breath, and Michael Muhammad Knight guided her hand to his junk. Some guys yelled shit like "*Daaaaaaamn!*" and the author kept the show going with his hands on two girls and the strawberry blond stroking him. She wanted it out but couldn't manage the buckle on his belt. He pulled his mouth away to explain that it came from the Portuguese infantry. He undid the buckle, the strawberry blond unzipped his pants, and they kissed while the brunette went down. He heard Amazing Ayyub and the teenage boys yell some more. Someone threw a cup of beer at the author and his girls but missed and hit the wall. Still busy, Michael Muhammad Knight waved a middle finger for the boys.

It worked out as an allegory from the Lord of the Worlds himself: the cigarette-breathed brunette with his piece in her mouth representing this filthy world, duniya, while the Bacardi-breathed strawberry blond kissing him symbolized higher aspirations of Allah's Nur, light within light and all that stuff. The kissing was only kissing and the blow job was lousy, so the author's ejaculation stemmed not from one girl in denial of the other but from both worlds, earthly and spiritual, in perfect harmony.

"That was the first time I've ever tasted it," said the brunette.

"I thought you had a boyfriend," replied Michael Muhammad Knight.

"I never got him off like that."

"So how'd you like your first shot?"

"It was all right. I don't know."

"How old do you think I am?" asked the strawberry blond.

"You're seventeen," he answered.

"Um, no."

"Sixteen?"

"I'm twelve."

"Bullshit."

"No, really. I'm twelve."

Michael Muhammad Knight looked at her for any sign that she'd undo the words. Then he looked at Amazing Ayyub and the drunk boys. They were all safe and had nothing to get scared about; their world was still the same as it had been a second ago.

Jail, thought the author.

She could have waved a loaded gun in his face and he wouldn't have been as scared. He looked at the brunette, who was struggling to hold back her laughter.

"Okay," he told the strawberry blond, "you're not twelve."

"Do you want to know how old I really am?"

"No."

"Don't worry about me," the brunette interjected. "I'm seventeen."

"I appreciate that."

Amazing Ayyub took his own slam-pig and fucked her in the bathroom. The high school boys stood by the door to hear it. Michael Muhammad Knight stayed on the couch with his two girls.

"It's too bad I'm on my period," said the strawberry blond. "We could have had a real threesome."

"I would have sex with you," said the brunette who had eaten his kids, "but I have a boyfriend."

"I understand," said the author. Ayyub's slam-pig came out naked and didn't care. She had a camera in her hands and wanted all the guys to get together for a picture, but nobody got up.

"I'm standing here fucking naked," she yelled. "I fuckin' shaved my snatch for you guys! I'll give everyone in here head if you just get in the fuckin' picture!" The high school boys all shouted their agreement, but the two old guys knew better than to let a drunken minor get them on film. Within ten minutes she was passed out anyway. They carried her to the couch, and one of the girls knew what to do in terms of tilting or not tilting her head back. Someone said to call 911, but the old guys weren't having that. Ayyub whispered to Michael Muhammad Knight that they should just drive her to the parking lot at Wegmans and leave her in a shopping cart. Eventually she came to and went back into the bathroom of her greatest triumph to throw up a little. Then she put on her clothes. After the high school boys cleared out, Michael Muhammad Knight and Amazing Ayyub drove the three girls to one of their houses.

As they pulled up to the curb, a porch light came on.

"*Shit!*"

"Don't worry," said Ayyub. "That's the neighbor's house."

"Oh, cool." Right when the brunette and the strawberry blond got their booze tramp out of the backseat, Michael Muhammad Knight slammed his foot on the gas. "This was no good," he whined. "This was no fucking good, bro."

"It's okay," said Ayyub.

"Man, what are you doing bringing girls like that over? The one tried telling me she was twelve."

"She wasn't twelve, bro."

"I know, man, but shit, how do I know? Who the fuck knows how old they are, they're fuckin' high school girls —"

"Did you tell them your real name?"

"I didn't tell them any name. I didn't get their names, either."

"Good. My name is Majestic, as far as they know."

"Majestic?"

"You never tell these sluts your real name."

"They were just in my fucking house!"

"They don't know their way around, bro. Not around our part of town, at least. If their moms knew that they were on Herman Street tonight, shit . . ."

Michael Muhammad Knight felt pretty bad the next day and even worse when those girls entered his masturbatory thoughts. He found an empty Bacardi bottle standing next to the couch. Assuming it had belonged to the strawberry blond, he scooped up the nearby cap as a souvenir. The cap had a picture of a bat on it, a reasonably wicked yet holy bat. A bat that knew too much. A Lucifer bat of worldly knowledge, but a Lucifer in the Nimatullahi sense, not the Judeo-Christian sense. An Iblis bat. Everything he did occurred beyond good and evil. People wouldn't want to pray behind him, but the bat had his role and he submitted to it like the sincerest of submitters. A paragon of love, the Bacardi bat.

Ayyub took a magazine into the bathroom. "Dropping the kids off at the pool," he called it. When he was done, he complained about having had the same old porn for too long; he said it was like being married for twenty years.

So Michael Muhammad Knight drove Ayyub down to American News and Video in the same torn-up, industrial part of town where they had shot off the fireworks.

This is Buffalo, thought the author. *These are the stories that you tell when you live in Buffalo.*

The porn shop had a big yellow sign reading American News and Video in sterile black letters. There was nothing sexy about the outside of the building—no neon lights, no silhouettes of female bodies—just plain placards that promised, in the same all-caps font, that you'd find DVDs, magazines, books, and novelties and could buy two videos at $19.99 each and get the third free.

Michael Muhammad Knight often felt carsick in porn shops. The whole store's worth of cheap graphics, bubblegum fleshy boxes, gaping vaginas, and fluorescent lights hit his eyes at once. He took a second to get over it. Then he walked around and had the same thoughts that everyone must have at some point in those places. You can't help but marvel at the sheer quantity of porn; even the thousands of films and photos in that store amounted to barely a drop in the filth sea. Then you consider the Internet, and the amateurs, and you wonder who these people are; there are so many of them, they have to be normal people. We wouldn't have a society if they weren't, and once you arrive at that, it just plain blows your mind.

Then you start to wonder what you'd do if you bought a porno and it showed your girlfriend or ex-girlfriend or mom or daughter getting trizzed by five cocks. Michael

Muhammad Knight had been in enough porn stores with enough college guys to hear the same question a thousand times: *What would you do?* As if there were anything *to* do. As if there'd be some action you could take.

He walked down the aisles of DVDs and knew enough to tell which ones were comedies and which were dramas. Some pornos were just meant to be bought as a joke and watched at a party: midget porn, really fat guys with little dicks, grandmother gang bangs, and so on. Others were so deeply serious that you watched them alone.

Michael Muhammad Knight whispered to Ayyub that the guy at the counter was watching them.

"I bet he thinks we're homos," said the Amazing One, who then turned and waltzed back out the door. The author followed him. Outside, Ayyub scurried around the parking lot, hunched over with his gaze lowered. "I'm lookin' for quarters," he said. "There's one!" He picked it up and they went back in. Ayyub headed straight for the video booths and knocked on a door.

"I think there's somebody in there," said the author.

"Oh," said Ayyub. He knocked on the door again. "Hey there, jerky! Heeeyyy! That's my quarter!" Then he wandered through the store, grabbing random boxes off the racks and mumbling, "Whore" when he felt like it.

"Where you boys from?" asked the guy at the counter.

"I'm from the land of filthy crotch," Ayyub answered.

"Aren't we all," said the guy. Ayyub studied a movie box in his hand.

"I WONDER IF THIS GIRL COULD FIT A BASE-BALL," he yelled. The author made his way to the other end of the store and picked up the box for a video titled *Just 18*. The pigtailed, plaid-skirted, topless girl on the cover had a cartoon-style word balloon next to her face in which she told him, "I've been a bad girl, so I deserve to be fucked by a scumbag like you!" He looked at her smile and pointy little tits and read it again.

A scumbag like you.

Michael Muhammad Knight returned *Just 18* to the rack and moved on, eventually finding himself in the same aisle as Amazing Ayyub.

"Let's get the fuck out of here," said the author.

"Yeah, bro." Ayyub said, "Have a good one" to the clerk.

When they were in the car and the author had turned on the ignition, Ayyub jumped back out. "Keep the car running," he said.

"What are you doing?" asked Michael Muhammad Knight.

"The Greater Jihad, bro. Jihad against yourself."

Amazing Ayyub grabbed a stick off the ground. It looked like it could have been a table leg. He stood statuesque for a moment in his bright orange fleece, Nautica splashed across his chest over skin that read Karbala, turned to his right—scouting for witnesses, maybe, or mouthing a silent salam to the angel on his shoulder—turned to the left, gave salam to that one, too, approached the store, raised the stick, and brought it crashing down through the window.

"THAT'S FOR MAKING ME JERK OFF ALL THE TIME!"

He dropped the stick and raced back to the car. Michael Muhammad Knight didn't know what to do but floor it out of the parking lot. The guy behind the counter came out just in time to see them flying down the road.

"WHAT THE SHIT WAS THAT?" screamed the author.

"That fag had it coming. He had those fuckin' movies in there with the guy who had two cocks and the other guy who stuck his dick in his own ass—that's not right."

"So you broke his window?"

"They shouldn't be showing that stuff, bro. That shit'll mess you up on the inside."

"Christ, Ayyub!"

"*Double-Dong Brothers*, that's what they called it."

"I bet that dude's pretty pissed about his window, anyway."

"I took that fucker out for the good of mankind. That's Progressive Islam, right?"

"Sure."

"Porn's no good, brother. There was this girl on one of the boxes in there, you know, I'd go in 'er with a speculum."

"What's a speculum?"

"I don't know, bro. But I would."

They drove back to Herman Street and parked the Skylark behind the house. It was a slow climb up the back porch. Michael Muhammad Knight opened the door, and they entered the house through his bedroom, passing shelves stocked with *Muhammad Entering from the Rear*.

A week later, they went back to American News and Video and observed that the outsides of porn shops looked extra sketchy in the daytime. They didn't go inside; they were just there to see the window. It had been covered up with a yellow placard warning that the area was under camera surveillance. There was still broken glass on the pavement.

They drove to Buffalo State College so Michael Muhammad Knight could check his email in the library. He received an invitation to attend a retreat in Garrison, New York: "Muslim Leaders of Tomorrow," they called it, promising a "dynamic group of American Muslims who are emerging leaders in a wide variety of professions." Michael Muhammad Knight wasn't sure if he had earned his spot by writing butt-sex novels or taking the janitorial world by storm.

Someone else wrote to him and asked what a book like *Muhammad Entering from the Rear* could do for the community.

Michael Muhammad Knight replied that the community could go fuck itself, adding that he'd rip out Farid Esack's liver and eat it. The community had enough writers pooping out their uplifting new visions of Islam, their twenty-first-century Islam, their American Islam. Their back-cover blurbs always promised a *refreshing* and *courageous* and *tolerant* and *modern* take on *the world's fastest-growing religion*, but that whole scene was a soulless academic circle jerk, as far as Michael Muhammad Knight could see.

As a writer he was okay, albeit a little crass at times and indulgent to the point that he started naming fictional characters after himself. Fiction was almost a form of hijab, since authors could write all the pervy stuff they wanted but still guard their Islamic modesty behind a made-up protagonist. Michael Muhammad Knight didn't have any Islamic modesty left to guard, so out with it . . .

By a conservative estimate, he owed the Creator of the Universe roughly 49,640 missed rakats, and the ticker was still running. He made out with one girl while another sucked him off. He did a girl in the ass to feel better about himself—and then written about it. Michael Muhammad Knight used to ride his bike to Canada for hookers. He once stole a Qur'an from the library because it was the Penguin edition and was spelled "Koran"; being fifteen and stupid, he thought he should remove it because the Penguin people obviously had no respect for Islam. But in later years he burned Qur'ans, he pissed on Qur'ans. He tossed one off a bridge into a creek, and for some reason, he buried one. His siratul-mustaqeem had become full of weeds and had grass growing in the tire ruts; it looked less like a road every year.

At least he wasn't the hero of his own story. Michael Muhammad Knight watched Ayyub sleeping on the couch—Ayyub, who he called Amazing and who underaged girls called Majestic. Ayyub couldn't do anything without somehow seeming violent about it, but that all left his face when he slept. The stench of his boots mingled with the living room's old-sperm smell. Ayyub was too pure to ever write a book.

Your Muslim Leader of Tomorrow left him and fell asleep in a bed.

RABEYA 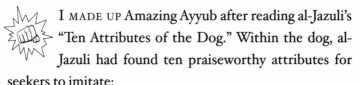 MATT DAMON

I MADE UP Amazing Ayyub after reading al-Jazuli's "Ten Attributes of the Dog." Within the dog, al-Jazuli had found ten praiseworthy attributes for seekers to imitate:

1. He sleeps only a little at night; this is a sign of the lovers of God (muhibbin).
2. He complains of neither heat nor cold; this is a sign of the patient (sabirin).
3. When he dies, he leaves nothing behind which can be inherited from him; this is a sign of the ascetics (zahidin).
4. He is neither angry nor hateful; this is a sign of the faithful (mu'minin).

5. He is not sorrowful at the loss of a close relative, nor does he accept assistance; this is a sign of the secure (muqinin).

6. If he is given something, he consumes it and is content; this is a sign of the contented (qani'in).

7. He has no known place of refuge; this is a sign of the wanderers (sa'ihin).

8. He sleeps in any place that he finds; this is a sign of the satisfied (radiyin).

9. Once he knows his master, he never hates him, even if he beats or starves him; this is a sign of the knowers ('arifin).

10. He is always hungry; this is a sign of the virtuous (salihin).

Sometimes I'll be a fictional character and also the faceless narrator, then step back and speak of myself in the first person, like this, as the human writer. Writers are always putting themselves in their stories and having conceited dialogues with their imaginary friends. In fact, it's very Christian to think of yourself as the god of your diegesis and then manifest yourself among its little men. It's embarrassing; an Islamically grounded author ought to keep the wall up.

I never really wrote *Muhammad Entering from the Rear*, but in the winter of 2002 I did write a novel about taqwacores — lunatic Muslim punk rockers — and starting out I really did make copies at Kinko's and hand them out for free. The spiral-bound taqwacore fantasy was supposed to be my farewell to Islam, a vomiting-up of all my religious failures with an added sliver of hope that someday it'd be all right, but then the book introduced me to some real-life Muslim misfits and I found a place for myself. Eventually it looked like we really could make a whole new scene of believers, half believers, and ex-believers calling ourselves and each other Muslims and starting punk bands. There was this Iranian shroom-head kid out in San Antonio who thought that the novel was a true story, so he emailed me asking if I could put him in touch with Amazing Ayyub and Rabeya the niqabi riot grrrl. The kid ended up starting his own band, Vote Hezbollah, named after a band from the book.

In Lowell, Massachusetts, there was Basim Usmani, who I had dreamed of long before ever knowing that he was real, that the world actually had mohawked Muslim punk singers. I dreamed of him praying the way Muslims pray but using a spread-out, dirty American flag for his prayer rug, and I dreamt of the tall spikes in his mohawk forming Arabic letters to spell "Allah": alif lam lam ha . . .

The real Basim was a goth/death-rock punk, while my dream Basim was a '77 Oi! punk named Jehangir who starred as the hero of my taqwacore novel. The fictional Jehangir had died in a mosh pit, and it looked like the real Basim might, too—a brown kid who went to white-power shows with the Pakistani flag painted on his leather jacket was just looking for trouble.

When the singer of Riff Raff (a "bald fat kid with a Henry Rollins complex," as Basim put it) jumped off the stage and started pushing people, microphone in hand, Basim was right there in front, and when the bald fat kid pushed him, he pushed back. Then the singer's brother yelled, "YOU LITTLE BITCH!" and punched Basim in the head. He fell behind a merchandise table and later regained consciousness to the taps and nudges of half a dozen boots. Someone yelled the old skinhead battle cry as Basim pulled himself up; he noticed that his left arm was flapping and held it to his chest. He staggered out and drove home, still not sure what had happened.

The assholes that night weren't Nazi but straightedge, which left Basim with an odd concept to explain to his mom: gangs of infidels who'd stomp a Muslim because they were opposed to drugs, alcohol, and premarital sex. "They kept me from desecrating my body," he explained.

First time I drove to Lowell and met Basim, he still had his arm in a sling, but I helped him to a vial of Hamza Yusuf's sweat that I had purchased at the last ISNA convention. Formerly Mark Hanson, Hamza Yusuf had left the fitna of surfing to become a shaykh and spread Allah's Nur across the world from his headquarters in Hayward, California. Shaykh Hamza can heal you, I told Basim, Shaykh Hamza can cure you, Shaykh Hamza can save you, and all we have to do is open up our hearts and our minds and let him in. After making proper niyya with a bismillah and throwing back the vial like a shot, Basim pulled off his sling to perform twenty-five push-ups and then a cartwheel.

Basim was in the process of starting a new band, a

taqwacore project called the Kominas, with this kid Shahjehan Khan who played on a guitar given to him by Salman Ahmad of Junoon, the biggest rock band in Asia. Shahjehan told me how for one show in Bangladesh with an audience of something like a hundred thousand people, Junoon was helicoptered down to a Hummer that drove the band to the stage, where they performed four or five songs before getting helicoptered away. Shahjehan was also good friends with Bilal Musharraf, whose father, Parvez, had become president of Pakistan in a 1999 military coup. Without approaching the right or wrong of overthrowing a government, I had to respect the balls it'd take to roll your dice like that. Made me wonder how Bilal had turned out, anyway. Sometimes we get our courage from our fathers because they give us shit to prove. My dad had never seized control of a third-world country, but he did manage to sleep with a woman while married to her daughter. Again, morals aside, at least respect the balls.

Shahjehan took us over to Bilal's condo; he ended up being just a really nice guy with a wife and a kid. His toddler, Hamza, ran around the house and sometimes looked at the Kominas and me as if we were aliens. I spotted President/ General Parvez in family portraits on the wall, just a proud grandfather holding baby Hamza, no military uniform or anything. While hanging with Bilal, we never mentioned his dad or got into politics. We did talk about Pakistan, but our discussion revolved mainly around geography. I told him about the places I had been to when I was a seventeen-year-old running around with the Tablighis.

After recording their first song, "Rumi Was a Homo (Wahhaj You're a Fag)," an attack on homophobic imam Siraj Wahhaj, the Kominas wanted to hit up a new mosque in Wayland that was still under construction, so we piled into the car. Singing along to whatever tapes he played, Basim redid Social Distortion's "Prison Bound" as "Jehennam Bound" and Judas Priest's "Breaking the Law" as "Pray to Allah" in his best Rob Halford, and I laughed so hard it hurt. I could have heard that all night: *Pray to Allah, pray to Allah! Pray to Allah, pray to Allah!*

The masjid was more or less just a huge wooden frame with no character yet, but once I was inside, I spotted the plywood mihrab showing the direction of Mecca. Otherwise, there was nothing that said "mosque." No pretty plaques, no wall hangings, no copies of the ISNA mag lying around, but we did have buckets of spackle and aluminum ladders. Off to the side, I saw what might be the sisters' entrance, Allah willing. We took a brief jaunt upstairs and walked past the beginnings of classrooms or offices. Shahjehan was smoking equality the whole time, but stayed respectful enough to step outside to dispose of it. Then the idea hit him to offer the first rakats in the history of the place. We looked around for something to pray on. There were sheets of plywood and one that had Keep Out! spray-painted on it, but Shahjehan found a big roll of insulation and unfurled it across the concrete. Basim went to take off his boots, but

I told him it wasn't necessary, that it was a tradition with no basis in anything. Shahj gave the adhan. I think it was Basim who wanted to pray without a leader, just the three of us going in unison. Sounded all right, but we each waited for someone else to start so we could synch up. Shahjehan took the initiative, said, "Allahu Akbar," and ended up as the de facto imam. I wasn't sure what prayer we were making; it was somewhere in the gray area between Isha time and Fajr. Could have gone either way, but Shahjehan stopped at two rakats, greeted the angels, and then spouted off some Arabic supplication that I had never heard before. I didn't know what he was saying, and maybe our weeded imam didn't know either, but it was about as sincere a prayer as I can get these days.

We took our final looks around, and Basim snatched up a handful of washers to make a necklace. Then we walked back through the mud and weeds to Basim's car. Basim drove me back to the T.J. Maxx where my Buick was parked, and I left him in his fearless taqwa-punk story: to live Jehennam-bound, start fights at shows, get drunk, and defend Islam against the sober. He's likely to die someday in a pit under the Doc Martens of one gang or another, and I think he knows it. Whatever the pen wrote, it wrote; there's not much else you can do.

The fiction now showed up on the nonfiction plane. Jehangir was fiction, but he put on a suit of flesh and now lived on as nonfiction Basim. Shahjehan was like a nonfiction version of my Yusef Ali character, the good kid who looked normal but didn't belong anywhere. Rabeya, probably the true hero of *The Taqwacores*, was inspired by a real girl I know. The real girl disappears from my life for months or even a year at a time, returns briefly, makes it emotionally intense, and then goes again, and I think it will be like that forever. She told me that someday she'll want a kid and pick me for the sperm donor, and I'll get to donate in the best way, and then she'll run off to raise the child in some women's commune in Afghanistan, and when the kid's fifteen or so, I'll be around to explain who I am.

After reading my punk novel, she told me that I was too passionate about my characters.

"You write like you're desperate to have these people remembered," she said, "and you don't have to; they're good characters. But once you've already described them, you describe them again. And you just push and push so hard to make them mean to the reader whatever they already mean to you."

"Sorry."

"Don't be sorry. Just know that you don't have to be afraid for them. They'll survive on their own."

Some of the characters were ugly. I wondered what kind of critique I'd get on pieces like my terrible "Shi'a Girl," in which a white convert punk hooks up with a desi girl and they have an argument because she doesn't think it's funny when Amazing Ayyub urinates into the drop box at a video store. The white convert punk was Michael Muhammad Knight, but I still wore the hijab of fiction, calling myself

Ben Majnun. In another story I made Ben Majnun the author of *Muhammad Entering from the Rear,* which he wrote by inserting a pen in his urethra and moving his lun across the page. "This of course requires an incredible amount of strength in that area," he'd tell girls at his readings; "I control muscles there that most men don't even know that they have."

Recite! And your Lord is most bountiful. He who teaches by the Pen, teaches man that which he knows not.
—Qur'an, 96:3–5

Ben's pen was his penis, and he could break it down: *My pen is my penis. My penis, my pen is.* See? Allah gives signs to those with understanding.

He had a whole process to it, beginning with a stainless-steel medical sound all KY'd up. First he'd use a thin sound, then one a little wider. After the third-level sound, he'd be ready for a pen. He bought his sounds from a medical-fetish website that also offered stethoscopes, latex gloves, sundry jars, hospital gowns, nurses' uniforms, straitjackets, stretchers, forceps, and enema equipment.

Ben's gift made him the male equivalent of a woman with no gag reflex, or a contortionist who could stick her feet behind her head—girls wondered what they could do with him. Imagine a real guy with a real piece who could move inside you in all the crazy ways sex-shop ticklers and battery-operated monsters did. A common misconception was that Ben's writing technique afforded him sexual plea-sure; apparently, some guys did insert things in their dicks for fun. All kinds of perverts approached Ben at readings and book signings, asking him how wide a sound he could fit and how many inches he went in. Ben would tell them to fuck off, as he found the whole thing incredibly pain-ful. One guy assumed that Ben's urethra was always wide enough to accommodate a pen and asked if he could look inside it, "to see what's up there." For some, Ben Majnun's penis was a gateway to self-knowledge.

As a literary talent, however, his lun was only so-so. It couldn't produce what you'd call a plot-driven story. You might expect a better sense of the narrative triangle: initial conflict, rising action, climax, falling action, return to equi-librium, and so on; but in reality, it just pounded away until the payoff.

I can't even read the Ben Majnun stories anymore, they're so bad, but this was how "The Shi'a Girl" ended:

He later called Sumayya and told her that after all his fits and starts of Gutter Sufism and full-blown apostasy, he was beginning to identify as a Shi'a.

"That's great! You need to make taqlid."

"Taqlid?"

"And you need to follow a qualified jurist."

"What the fuck are you talking about?"

"And you need to find someone living to follow."

"For what?"

"I suggest either Ayatollah Sayyed Seestani or Ayatollah Bayyed Ali Khamenaie."

"The both of them can eat it."

"But if you're Shi'a, you need a guide."

"Do these fuckfaces guide you to spill Bacardi all over yourself and grind up on guys in the club?"

"Fuck you!" she cried. She hung up, and that was it for her.

Back to Amazing Ayyub, whom I've now placed in California:

Amazing Ayyub the Iranian Shiite Skinhead couldn't have weighed more than a buck fifty, but he had the wiry survival strength of an animal that's always hungry but still has to run and fight and keep its eyes open and never sleep. No fat on his body, and no inch of his skin without detail—poor Ayyub was all scars, veins, bones, and Karbala tattoo. No shirt, and he drove his van like that same crazed animal, squeezing hard on the wheel, elbows locked, pulling insane but controlled swerves across lanes. He had his Sham 69 coming in loud from the one working speaker and he had those streets owned, and riding in back he had Rabeya the punk niqabi sitting on a stolen amp and pointing an AK-47 in the direction of a tied-up Matt Damon. Behind Damon hung a Saudi flag with a red anarchy sign spray-painted on the Kalimah. These were the taqwacores who passed the frontiers of all reasonable religion, serving Islam in exile, trying to realize the imams of their inner being while saying "fuck all" to the rest of it.

Holding the AK with one hand, ninja-looking Rabeya

reached with the other into the folds of her black cloak and pulled out her phone. "Turn the radio down," she told Ayyub; she had demands to make.

"Listen up," she told someone on the other end. "We have Matt Damon and we're gonna blow his head off unless you fulfill our demands!

"What we demand is for Hollywood to give a positive depiction of Muslims, just one movie where we're not these two-dimensional Al-Qaeda stereotypes! No more of this *Delta Force* bullshit, you hear me?"

"And no more *Sum of All Fears!*" shrieked Ayyub from the front. "Tom Clancy can suck my cock!"

"No more *True Lies*," continued Rabeya, "no more *Siege*, no more fucking *Executive Decision* or *Rules of Engagement*. No more *Not Without My Daughter*—I mean, the story was valid, but what if it was the other way around and showed this asshole Amer—But anyway, listen! One decent movie in which Muslims are reasonable human beings, or we kill Matt Damon!" She hung up and let them think about it.

"So you guys are Muslim, I imagine," said Damon, perfectly calm.

"That's right," replied Rabeya. "Nothing personal against you, you know—you're just a way to get these guys' attention."

"In that case, as-salam alaikum."

"Wa alaikum as-salam," she answered.

"I've gotta tell you," said Matt Damon, "I'm worried about you guys falling into your own cliché stereotype here."

"FUCK YOU, MATT DAMON!" screamed Amazing Ayyub. "TAKBIR!"

"Allahu Akbar," said Rabeya.

"Don't get me wrong," said Damon. "I completely sympathize with your grievance. Hollywood's depiction of Muslims has been erroneous and utterly shameful. I'm just afraid that by taking a hostage, you're playing into that same terrorist paradigm and furthering a neoconservative perception of Islam."

"What's a neoconservative?" asked Ayyub.

"Not to mention," Damon continued, "there's no basis in the Qur'an, nor the Sunnah, for you to take an innocent person hostage."

"Fuck it," said Rabeya, lowering the gun. "I think Matt Damon's right."

"Now, Amazing Ayyub," said Damon, "I noticed that your tattoo says Karbala. Are you Shi'a?"

"Yeah, bro."

"So you adhere to the infallible example set by the Twelve Holy Imams."

"Fuckin' A."

"Then you must be aware that the Fifth and Sixth Holy Imams both opposed armed rebellion."

"No shit?"

"No shit."

With all the rusty, dusty mystique of a *Mad Max* archetype, haggard and worn after driving all the way from his postbellum nightmare, Amazing Ayyub pulled into the

Mobil station and hopped out to pump gas. Still shirtless, he went in to pay, leaving Matt Damon, Rabeya, and her AK-47 in the van. The van had gone nine thousand miles with him and had been through enough to become a character in the story, too. It was in this van that Ayyub carted taqwacore bands like the Mutaweens, Vote Hezbollah, and Osama Van Halen on their tours. The stolen amp was revenge after that show in Oakland when the club owner had stiffed the Gandoos out of their money. Those bands were genuine taqwa-punks and did it only for the taqwa, nothing else.

No sign of the clerk anywhere, so Ayyub ripped open a Twix and smashed both bars into his mouth. Before even swallowing, he did it again with a 3 Musketeers, then attacked a Reese's. He smeared the mess of chocolate, peanut butter, and saliva on his face onto his bare forearm and left the wrappers on the floor. He looked at the magazines, tearing open the plastic sheath on a *Penthouse*. Then he picked up the glossy music mag *Punk Press*, and it drilled him like a Shawn Michaels superkick to the chin: On the front cover were four pretty, clean desi boys with piercings and sleeve tattoos, one wearing a Vote Hezbollah T-shirt for underground cred. Off to the side, it read: "Shah 79: Godfathers of Muslim Punk."

"Are you fuckin' kidding?" scoffed Ayyub, loud enough for anyone in the place to hear, but there was still nobody there. "Look at this slick shit," he mumbled, flipping the pages until he found those douchebags again. They had a whole spread, with more cool poses and a rundown of who in the group got wasted and who didn't ("Javed has never had a beer in his life, but Omar will party his tits off"), and what a hard time they'd had recording their new album ("I wanted the song to be this intricate Sufi allegory, you know, but Omar thought it was about a girl"). One of the pussies had a line about aiming for the moon because if you missed, you'd land among the stars. Another showed off the bismillah inked around his neck and said, "Like my tattoos, my heart hurts for Allah." Amazing Ayyub had never heard of them, and they didn't look like anything that would have cruised around in his terrible van—their magazine faces were too soft and well rested to have ever suffered a real taqwa road war with Ayyub behind the wheel. The taqwacores were Gutter Sufi heroes; these kids were a new breed, weak and grafted from the original.

Could it be?

Taqwacore . . . *pop*-punk?

Ayyub threw down the rag and still couldn't find a clerk, so he just walked back out, cursing Shah 79 and shouting that Rabeya wouldn't believe that shit . . .

But the van was gone.

Ayyub looked in every direction and made a quick lap around the Mobil, then ran up the street and turned to look the other way. He figured that he had probably taken too long in there looking at magazines and stealing candy, causing Rabeya to get scared and bust out of there for the good of the mission. Or maybe Matt Damon had pulled some

Hollywood heroics, gotten himself loose, and overpowered her—but fuck no, Rabeya had had that AK on him and wouldn't have had any doubts about pulling the trigger. But Ayyub hadn't heard the gun. Only other thing he could think of was that the cops had shown up and Rabeya had peeled out. They could be chasing her down the freeway right then, with helicopters overhead and everything. Walking back toward the Mobil, Amazing Ayyub had nowhere to go, but he knew that in such a scenario he had to at least leave the scene. He stood over the fresh oil-leak puddle where the van had just been, thanked Allah that Rabeya at least had a free tank of gas on her side, said a quick Al Fatiha for her sake, and then strolled down the sidewalk—no sprint, no panic.

Less than a mile down the street, he went behind a bowling alley and sat down with his back against the wall. He wondered what the odds might have been that Rabeya was driving up I-5 with a bloody Matt Damon corpse, and joked to himself about its coming alive. Zombie Matt Damon, ha ha. Then he thought about Shah 79 again. Godfathers of Muslim punk? "More like cocksuckers of Muslim Punk," he said out loud, wishing that someone were around to laugh at it.

Fuckin' Shah 79, cocksuckers of Muslim Punk—look at those guys with their skateboarding T-shirts; you know they're biting the pillows for somebody . . .

What was happening? Had Muslim cool taken over? Was Shah 79 showing up on MTV with green taqwa laces in their Docs? Ayyub didn't have anything to say, beyond "fuck 'em." After just sitting behind the bowling alley for a while, he got up and walked to the Greyhound station, bought a ticket to Santa Cruz, and gave his last quarter to the *Galaga* machine.

When he got off the bus, he slumped down behind a Dumpster and knocked out for a while. When he woke up, his eyes felt like they were sealed shut, but he rubbed them hard and opened them up to the sun, and the first thought in his head was Shah 79, those fuckers—the great betrayal. He got up and scouted around the parking lot for proper materials to pull off a curse. To do Hakim Bey's Malay Black Djinn Curse, he'd need a hard-boiled egg, along with three iron pins and an iron nail to stick in it, a dried scorpion, a lizard and/or beetles, a small chamois bag of cemetery dirt, magnetized iron filings, asafetid, and sulfur. He'd sew the charm into yellow silk and place everything in a bottle, then cork it and seal it with wax. Hakim Bey claimed that the curse was useful for dealing with evil institutions.

While Amazing Ayyub was hunting for magical items in a Santa Cruz parking lot, Michael Muhammad Knight was in Buffalo, wanting to warn him that the energy in western New York was bad, and that he'd better not come back. The Buffalo news reported that an unidentified man in his late teens to mid-twenties had been found dead by the railroad tracks. If you know a guy like Amazing Ayyub, you get scared at every story like that, because it could so easily be him. Even with Ayyub in California, Michael still called the Buffalo Police Department to see if the body wore Karbala on its chest. Poor Amazing Ayyub, kullu ardh'n Karbala; Michael Muhammad Knight wanted to give him a ring like the one worn by his Sixth Holy Imam, Jafar as-Sadiq, reading: Allah is my master and my defense from his creation. There was so much evil around Ayyub, and he didn't even know yet . . . and even with the ring, the Sixth Imam was killed off with poisoned grapes.

Ayyub discovered the news of a taqwacore after venturing beyond the parking lot and reading the flyer on a telephone pole. It could have meant a chance to find places to crash or maybe a ride somewhere. He ripped the flyer off the pole and kept walking.

The sad and terrible fact of taqwacore was that it put Muslim kids in kafr bars, but Hafiz said that the time for judging sober and drunk and far and near has passed, and the Sixth Holy Imam said that you cannot expect your children to do things as you did, takbir takbir takbir. The first band that night was classic California taqwa-punk, Muhammad Muzammad, which looked less like a band than like a gang— just three brown kids wearing their mohawks the same way, like the broom atop a Roman gladiator's helmet, thousands of Aqua Netted bristles giving the illusion of a single, solid ornament upon the scalp. The guitarist's was pink, the bass player's was green, and the drummer's was yellow. The guitar and bass players hopped and moved the same way. At one point the guitar player and the singer said something along the lines of "Fuck Shah 79, fuck that bullshit!" and Ayyub screamed his approval with the cool kids. It didn't even hit Ayyub that the cool kids were really *kids* and he wasn't, that he was living on borrowed time when it came to anything that could be called youth culture.

Second band was the Zaytuna Rejects: four more brown boys, heroin-skinny, with sleeveless shirts and spiked bracelets loose on their wrists, the singer holding his drink and spilling beer as he slouched behind the microphone, working this detached, crooner-punk style like he was too cool to care either way. When he really got going, though, he got good, entering into crazy fits as if he were fighting three invisible cops. Sometimes it looked like the cops were winning, but then he'd fight his way through them. For most of his songs, the kids in the crowd stood still with their hands in their pockets, but by the time he whipped out his sing-along anthem, he had them bouncing around with their arms around each other. "Fuckin' A!" yelled Ayyub. A lone Mohican from Muhammad Muzammad, the back of his vest covered in thousands of even-columned spikes, stood on the outer edge of the audience and nodded from his authority.

The band that followed the Zaytuna Rejects wasn't even punk as such; it was more death metal than anything, but the taqwacores still loved it; they started pits and climbed onstage to jump back off into the waiting chaos. The band sported classic metal hair, wore all black, and even had a metal-sounding name: Zulfikar, after the mythical sword of the Prophet. The meaning of Zulfikar was read as "the one who distinguishes between right and wrong" or, alternately, "cleaver of the spine," for legend said that a single blow from the blade would split a person right down the middle, clean in half. The Prophet had first picked up Zulfikar as booty from the Battle of Badr. He'd bequeathed the sword to Imam Ali, who in turn had left it to his son Husain, who'd died with it in his hands on the terrible battlefield of Karbala. Despite Zulfikar's metal pretenses, Amazing Ayyub liked it best out of all the bands because it was so openly Shi'acore and bellowed death-rock songs about the final battle between Mahdi and Dajjal. The entire band looked buff enough to be on steroids, and the singer's torso resembled an upside-down pyramid: massive shoulders, massive lats, and no waist at all. On his bare chest, he wore a tattoo of the sword Zulfikar. Spread across his broad back was a lion composed of elaborate Arabic calligraphy. The lion was an elegant manipulation of words, most likely holy words, words praising Allah or His Prophet or the Prophet's House. The singer's long hair was dyed blond, but he kept his thick beard black.

Like the other bands, Zulfikar reassimilated into the audience after its set. Amazing Ayyub found his way over to the singer, and they simultaneously noticed each other's chests: the Zulfikar singer with his long curvy Ali sword, Amazing Ayyub with his old-English Karbala. Without any words beyond smiling salams, they embraced, automatic brothers.

"What's that lion say on your back?" asked Ayyub, turning the singer around so he could see it again.

"La fata illa Ali, la saif illa Zulfikar," answered the singer. "There is no hero except Ali, no sword except Zulfikar."

"That's tits, bro," said Ayyub. "You don't see a lot of Shi'a taqwa-punk bands out here. There was this one I saw in L.A.—I don't even remember their names but the dudes were fuckin' slicing their arms up with razor blades and crying and going nuts."

"There are different ways to manifest your love for the Ahlul-Bayt," replied the singer, coming off almost as a professor. Ayyub looked at the guy's forehead and spotted those deep old scars, even in the darkness. The singer saw the same razor-blade road map on Ayyub. They caught each other looking. "We're serious on our shit," said the singer. Ayyub nodded.

Later, it was Ayyub and the singer sitting on the curb outside the bar, each of them with a brown bottle, the show still going on inside.

"D'you hear about these Shah 79 fags?" asked Ayyub.

"Yeah," replied the singer. "It's all about selling a watered-down deen to the kafirun."

"Fuck 'em," said Ayyub.

"They're changing Islam to make it soft and safe. They're cutting our balls off."

"I don't know who these fuckers are."

"You should," said the singer. "That's your scene."

"What the fuck are you talking about?"

"Shah 79? They're from your neck of the woods, y'akhi. Buffalo."

"Those cocksuckers are from Buffalo?" The singer realized the weight of Ayyub's discovery and kept his mouth shut. Ayyub stood up, unsure of what choice he could make with his body at that moment, wishing there was a movement right then and there that he could offer to destroy Shah 79, but all he could do was grip his bottle by the neck and whip it into the air. The bottle sailed in a high arc and went far enough for its crash to make almost a gentle sound. "That's some bullshit," Ayyub said. He repeated himself a few times. "Fuckin' . . . how did that happen, bro?"

"They weren't always Shah 79," said the singer, still sitting on the curb. "They used to call themselves the Black Box Khatibs."

"What does that mean?"

"You know what a black box is, like on a plane? So they were the khatibs, giving khutbahs into a black box. Think about it, bro."

"Jesus," said Amazing Ayyub.

"I don't agree with the reference, personally. Rasullullah sallallaho alayhe wa salam did not teach the taking of innocent lives. But those kids, at least they had the balls to do their shit and really mean it. Now they're just pussies."

"Buffalo—I can't believe it. Buffalo was no joke when I was there. Shit . . ."

"It's a joke now."

"I'm going back. These Walden Galleria punks don't

know how it used to be! I can set 'em straight; I'm like a fuckin' legend out there. They'll know who I am. I can tell them about the old days and, shit, I don't know, turn it around."

"If you need to go east," said the singer, "you can ride with us. We're playing shows all the way to the coast. You can drive the van and work our merch table."

"A-plus, bro. I'm the fastest driver in the whole history of taqwacore."

So when the show ended and the kids poured out of the bar, Amazing Ayyub and the singer reunited with the rest of Zulfikar, and Ayyub introduced himself as their new roadie. They seemed like emotionally intense guys. Ayyub helped them load their amps and stuff into the van and volunteered to drive. They all piled in; the singer rode shotgun.

All they had in the way of tapes was death metal, and Ayyub grew tired of it, turning off the music once the whole band was asleep. He floored it through the night, making hundreds of miles and getting them all the way from the coast to the state line and into Nevada. At one point, the singer woke up and told Ayyub that the First Imam, Ali bin Abu Talib, knew what awaited him, so he said that his future assassin should be killed only with a stroke equal to what he himself had suffered. And the First Imam forbade the mutilation of dead bodies, as he had heard the Prophet say, "Mutilate not even a dead dog."

"That's for real," said Ayyub.

"That's the kind of thing we need to remember, brother."

"Yeah."

"Brother, we have to remember it when that yahooda bitch kills the Mahdi."

"Yahooda?"

"She's already out there. Didn't you hear about that? A few years back, Ayatollah Behjat's giving a lecture, and out of nowhere he just starts weeping. So the students ask him what's wrong, and he says he just had a vision: He saw the yahooda girl being born in Isfahan who's gonna grow up and martyr Mahdi."

"Are you serious?"

"I shit you not, brother. The Twelfth Imam's killer is already here. You think we lift weights to look good onstage? It's going down soon enough." With that, the singer closed his eyes again, leaving Ayyub alone to think about it.

The next morning in Buffalo, Michael Muhammad Knight woke up and went to the abandoned car in the backyard. Instead of a sleeping Amazing Ayyub, all he found in the passenger seat was a mess of spit-out date pits. Michael Muhammad Knight thought of a quote to sum up Amazing Ayyub, lowest of the low:

> *Do you want to be a pilgrim on the path of love? The first step is making yourself as humble as ashes.*
>
> —Ansari of Herat

And for himself:

You don't realize that what I am doing here is the last tired effort of a man who once did something finer and better.

—F. Scott Fitzgerald

The doghouse in the backyard was unpainted, still only the color of ugly, plain wood, and the author had filled it with old wrestling dolls, the classic 1980s LJN line: Hulk Hogan; Big John Studd; George "The Animal" Steele, with his green tongue sticking out; Superfly Snuka, from the Fiji Islands, in leopard-print trunks; Junkyard Dog, with THUMP emblazoned across his ass; the Iron Sheik, with his sinister, curly-toed boots; Hillbilly Jim, with that big bushy beard that could make him a Taliban if you covered his blue overalls with a jalab; Kamala the Ugandan Giant, with bare feet and a moon on his belly; Corporal Kirschner, the camouflaged and dog-tagged semijobber; the devious Mr. Fuji, in tuxedo and bowler hat . . . the author had them all standing together in rows reaching to the back of the doghouse. He looked at what he had done, how the dolls stood with each other, brother by brother, in straight and even rows.

The figures needed an imam. Andre the Giant seemed the safest choice; he was far and away the greatest man among them, and a hafiz in Michael's imagination. The way Andre's figure was posed with his hands up by his head looked the closest to prayer position, anyway. Allahu Akbar—too bad the rubber figures weren't posable and had to make salat in fixed bicep poses and grappling stances. Who prayed like that? Maybe the Druzes. At least Tito Santana had his arms at his sides, his hands open like a Shi'a's, but he was naked, save for his skimpy purple trunks and knee-high wrestling boots.

Michael Muhammad Knight half hoped for some *Indian in the Cupboard*-type magic. Perhaps he'd come back the next morning and find a halaqa going on, Hulk Hogan discussing the Qiyama as though hyping a *Saturday Night's Main Event* show: "WELL, YA KNOW SOMETHING, BROTHER," he'd bellow, gruff and amped, with Mean Gene holding the microphone to his face, "WHAT ALLAH'S TRYING TO SAY HERE IS, WHATCHA GONNA DO WHEN THE EARTH SPILLS FORTH WHAT IT CONTAINS? AND WHATCHA GONNA DO WHEN THE MOUNTAINS CRUMBLE? AND WHATCHA GONNA DO WHEN THE QIYAMA RUNS WILD OVER YOU?" Michael Muhammad Knight, unaware that Ayyub now roamed with an apocalyptic Shi'a metal band that was busy preparing for such things, wondered what Amazing Ayyub would do when the mountains became like carded wool and Ya'jooj and Ma'jooj were let loose to rush headlong down the hills.

Ayyub was a barbarian champ anyway, hunting his food in Buffalo winter year after year. One night he'd stolen a bag of shrimp from the nontraditional students' lounge at Buffalo

State College. At Herman Street he'd cooked the goods in Michael Muhammad Knight's microwave and served them in hot dog rolls with ketchup. It was just about the most depressing meal the author had ever had, especially when Ayyub went off on his brilliant money schemes. The first was to save up a sizable chunk of cash, a couple thousand dollars or so, and then drive with it across the bridge to Niagara Falls, where he'd exchange it for Canadian quarters. He'd take the quarters all rolled up to someplace far from the border like Colorado and then trade them for bills. The bank teller, assuming that the rolled quarters are American, will give you American bills. Depending on the exchange rate when you did it, you could make a good profit.

With that money, Ayyub announced, they'd bring a whore over and make her fuck herself with a wine bottle while they all masturbated to it. The author almost choked on his shrimp sandwich.

Ayyub's other big caper involved collecting those free credit cards that college-age people got in the mail all the time. Ayyub said he'd sign up for every last one and slowly build credit by buying little things like soda and magazines. Eventually, he'd get a mass of thirty to forty credit cards, and then he'd go down to New York and buy gold everywhere you could. When the bill collectors eventually came after him, he'd just declare bankruptcy and forget about them. They wouldn't be able to do anything to him because he'd have no money, just a secret trunk of gold buried in his backyard. He'd take all those necklaces he bought and melt 'em, and then he'd be rich. According to Ayyub, he could then hire a woman to fuck herself with a cucumber while he masturbated to it.

Michael Muhammad Knight did not masturbate to whores with cucumbers or wine bottles, but at the last ISNA convention he'd picked up the brochure from a shalwar kameez manufacturer and made repeated istimna to it in the bathroom. There were beautiful girls in that brochure with dark wet hair and long lashes, modeling silks with patterns that he thought he had seen on the outer walls of mosques in Isfahan. He kept the catalog as a memento of the convention, but felt creepier as it accumulated creases over time.

THE KOMINAS

PUNK-EATING ZOMBIES

 ZULFIKAR'S DRUMMER GAVE Amazing Ayyub enough speed and Stacker 2 to keep up his insane bouts of marathon driving through the desert, his eyes burning and his brain boiling but his grip on the wheel still tight and tense. Even drugged and wired, he fought to keep his eyes open and sometimes fell asleep, slowly lowering his head toward the dashboard and then violently jerking it back as he woke up. The band never noticed. The empty desert made Ayyub imagine them all to be living in another time, as though he were driving their van to ninth-century Samarra. He began to think of himself as their slave and felt it to be a holy position, since they were great soldiers for the Mahdi, in need of a chauffeur to martyrdom.

The Mahdi was the twelfth and last in that long line of

sufferers, the Holy Imams, waiting in ghaybat for the final confrontation with Dajjal, the Islamic Antichrist, who'd make his arrival near the end of the world. The band held firmly to a theory that the Dajjal was already here, as none other than the Taliban's Mullah Omar, since the hadiths had foretold that Dajjal would have only one eye.

The kings of Shi'a death metal were also hashishiyyas, clouding the van's inside with smoke as they discussed various fighting styles and the risks associated with excessive ejaculations: Sex takes away all of your power, said the bass player; it drains your male life force, and you really shouldn't chance it more than a couple of times a year. And there were serious spiritual dangers to it, anyway, he added. Before having sex with his wife, said the hadiths, a man should mention the name of Allah and take refuge from Shaytan—but if Allah were neglected, Shaytan would fold himself up in the man's penis and make it a threesome. In the heat of the moment, said the bass player, you could forget to remember your Creator, astaghfir'Allah. Amazing Ayyub kept his hurting eyes on the road and thought about his charlatan girls from over the years while the bass player continued with bad news: If you have sex with your wife while she's menstruating, Shaytan comes before you. Your offspring will then be a mukhannath, a sterile person, a child of the jinn.

While high, the singer liked to read from the Nahjul Balagha, the collected teachings of Ali, the First Holy Imam. The singer's copy had a green-and-black camouflage cover, bearing its title in classic stenciled army letters. He explained that the cover reminded him that Muslims were always in jihad against themselves and in that Greater Jihad, the Nahjul Balagha was the greatest weapon he could have.

The singer flipped to a random page and read: "If you desire I will tell you about Isa, son of Maryam. He used a stone for his pillow, put on coarse clothes, and ate rough food. His condiment was hunger. His lamp at night was the moon. His shade during the winter was just the expanse of earth eastward and westward. His fruits and flowers were only what grows from the earth for the cattle. He had no wife to allure him, nor any son to give grief, nor wealth to deviate his attention, nor greed to disgrace him. His two feet were his conveyance and his two hands his servant."

The rest of the band nodded their heads, mumbling comprehension and acceptance under their breaths.

"That's pretty fuckin' punk rawk," said Ayyub, behind the wheel.

The singer seemed to be the scholar and real thinker of the group. He not only read a variety of works but also produced his own ideas on them. He told everyone in the van how the Third Imam, Imam Husain, the Lion of Karbala, had married a Persian princess, giving the future Imams not only Prophet Muhammad's holy bloodline but also that of Iranian royalty. The Fourth Imam, Imam Ali Zainul-Abideen, son of Imam Husain and the Persian princess, was twenty-two years old when his father was decapitated, trampled under horses, and left to rot in the sun. And then the mantle was passed to him.

Zulfikar's lead singer explained that the Fifth Imam, Imam Muhammad al-Baqir, had a special place in the lineage. His mother, Fatima, was daughter of the Second Imam; his father, Ali, was son of the Third. Muhammad al-Baqir tied together the loose ends, having for his grandfathers both of the Prophet's beloved grandsons. The Fifth Imam was a walking marriage between the sacred twins (Hasan and Husain weren't really twins, but they fulfilled the archetype). Muhammad al-Baqir created brief symmetry in the Tree of Infallibles, with Hasan and Husain representing the median line between two halves. On one side was Prophet Muhammad, whose daughter Fatima married Ali. On the other side were Hasan's daughter Fatima and Husain's son Ali having a son named Muhammad. It was a completed cycle of creation and the kind of thing that'd move you when you heard about it in the endless Utah wasteland.

The singer then told Ayyub and the band that the Wahhabs wouldn't marry Shi'as or even let them rest in Wahhab cemeteries. At Jannat al-Baqi, Wahhabs destroyed the tombs of the Second, Fourth, Fifth, and Sixth Holy Imams. Ayyub had no response beyond "Fuck the Sauds, bro."

From the highway, Amazing Ayyub spotted a pair of long, thin minarets in the distance, so he pulled over and they all abandoned the van to hop a fence and walk to the mosque. Turned out to be farther away than it had first seemed, but interstate-side mosques possessed a certain magic worth chasing. Amazing Ayyub whipped open the heavy wooden doors, kicked off his boots, and strolled into the prayer hall without bothering to make wudhu, though he really owed ten thousand ghusls for his lifetime of masturbation in the bushes. While the members of Zulfikar took off their shoes and headed for the wudhu faucets, properly washing for prayer, Ayyub hung out by himself. The masjid was a wide-open space with tall ceilings, blank white walls, and large windows that washed the room in sunlight. The mihrab was simple but pretty, a niche of tiles bearing a verse of the Qur'an, framed all around by unreadable calligraphy. Thin strings running along the floor from one wall to the other indicated the proper spacings for rows of men. Ayyub turned from the mihrab and saw the balcony for women looming above.

He walked in large, unplanned circles across the big room, the carpet soothing his brutalized feet. Stepping into a mosque made him remember all the other mosques he had ever been to in his life, and a new seriousness slowly overtook him. Even without wudhu, being in a masjid washed off some of Ayyub's Ayyub-ness, and he became, if only for a relaxed moment, just another Muslim, Ayyub Masoom.

Ayyub noticed that he didn't have a shirt on and briefly felt bad about it, though there was no hadith or anything saying that he needed a shirt to pray. He looked over the scars on his torso and his arms, almost wishing that he remembered where they all came from but then letting the masjid feed a fantasy that he'd earned them in holy ways at Badr, that he was a 1,500-year-old mujahid ready to lie down in a mosque and die in his sleep. He actually did consider putting himself in a corner and passing out. Then he wondered what was taking Zulfikar so long; they had been making wudhu for a while.

Ayyub made half a lap around the room before finding a spot that felt right, stood to face the mihrab, made his niyya to pray two nafl rakats, and went to it—Allahu Akbar—putting his arms at his sides. He bent over, straightened up again, went to the floor, and rested his forehead on the carpet. During sujdah, Amazing Ayyub's whole forearms would touch the ground. In Islamic Sunday school, as a little junior Ayyub, he'd been taught that this in fact made for unacceptable practice. "That's how a dog lies," his teacher had told him.

Sitting in his final julus, his index finger moving up and down as he whispered the Tashahud under his breath, Ayyub heard something behind him: a distant shuffle, a step, a long, droning groan. *One of the guys from Zulfikar*, he thought, immediately regretting that he had taken that moment to be distracted. More shuffles, another groan, now coming closer. Ayyub wanted to turn around and see who it was, but he couldn't allow himself that physical departure from salat. As he neared the end of his prayer, at which point he'd turn to the right and left to greet the angels on his shoulders, the sounds advanced directly behind him. Out of the corner of his eye, he saw it and jumped to his feet.

It was a man, a middle-aged Arab with a full Salafi beard and a long white jalab, his chest covered in dried blood from a gaping wound on his neck that caused his head to lean to the other side. His stare was frozen, completely vacant, with no direction at all. His skin was ashy and pale. He moved slowly toward Amazing Ayyub, dragging one foot and then the other.

"Salam alaik," said Ayyub. The man groaned. Ayyub caught the man's stench and backed up. The man made another step and almost looked like he'd fall. "You all right, bro?" Ayyub asked. The man groaned again and raised his hands for Ayyub's throat. "I'M NOT A HOMO!" Ayyub screamed, slapping him away. The man gave no acknowledgment, only groaned and reached again. Ayyub was trembling, his fists cocked so tight that his fingertips could push through his palms. "Yo, step off," he warned, his voice quivering. "I'll fucking stab you in the head." The Arab let out a long, soft, nearly sensual groan. It was the last straw for Ayyub, who then hauled off and punched him in the jaw. It didn't do a thing. The Arab moaned, opened his mouth wide, and lunged at Ayyub, who exploded with a flurry of rights and lefts and kicks to the nuts before getting away. The man was still standing, still groaning and moaning, still wanting Ayyub. When the members of Zulfikar finally came into the masjid, Ayyub was so vexed that he couldn't even notice their empty, glazed-over eyes, tilted heads, gaping mouths, and open, bloody wounds. "We gotta get the fuck out of here," Ayyub told them. "This is one of those Progressive mosques." The members of Zulfikar moved on him with the same shuffling steps as the Arab;

at first it looked like they'd help Ayyub beat the shit out of the Arab, but then their blood-crusted hands reached for Ayyub. "WHAT THE SHIT?" he screamed, his voice cracking, the words pushing themselves violently out of him. Zulfikar now stood between Amazing Ayyub and the door, causing him to back up toward the mihrab, where he bumped into the Arab. Then they all swarmed him, the Arab and the feral-haired Shi'a metal band, all at once, Ayyub responding with a spasm of indiscriminate violence, punching and kicking until he could break out and catch some distance. Ayyub bolted for the door, his slow pursuers shuffling behind him, when from above came a world-annihilating thunder of noise and the Zulfikar drummer's head exploded. While the rest of them continued their plodding march toward Ayyub, he looked at the drummer standing there headless, blood sprayed all around him, chunks of brain and skull decorating the mosque's floor. The drummer dropped to his knees, his body remaining stiffly upright for a moment before falling forward, finished. Another blast from above hit the singer, shattering his left shoulder but failing to stop him. Amazing Ayyub looked up to the women's balcony and saw taqwacore hero Basim Usmani, singer of the Kominas, in black vinyl pants and a shirt of metallic latex body paint, pumping his shotgun. Basim took aim and blew the Arab's head clean off, then jumped over the balcony's railing and fell some twenty feet to the masjid floor, landing like a cat, shotgun still in hand. He rose to his feet and let out a shot that exploded the bassist's skull, then fired twice into the guitar player's stomach. The guitar player kept coming, so Basim raised his aim to the man's head and pulled the trigger. Basim's body reacted to the shotgun in natural harmony, supporting and cradling the explosion in his arms without a flinch, as though the young man and his firearm were only cooperating parts of one machine. After shooting off the guitar player's head, a sudden sadness delayed Basim's next move. Momentarily forgetting that he still had the Zulfikar singer left, he watched a steady flow of blood pour from the guitar player's neckhole onto the masjid carpet. He studied the scattered bits of flesh and shattered chips of bone, the sprays of blood on the white mosque walls. Then he swung around to face the staggering singer, snarled, and pulled. The singer collapsed, his right leg blown off at the knee, but without hesitation began pulling himself toward Basim. Rather than waste further ammo on an attacker who could only crawl, Basim reached for the sheathed machete hanging off his back, pulled it out, and hacked at the singer's neck. There was no suffering beyond the denial of a hunger.

The heads of Ayyub's attackers were all severed or destroyed. "Thanks, bro," said Ayyub. "I tried telling that one dude that I wasn't a fuckin' homo. I could have handled him myself, but then these other guys . . . I don't know what happened, man! They were in a fuckin' metal band and I was driving their van. I didn't think they'd turn out like that."

"They weren't trying to have sex with you," said Basim.

"They were zombies. They overtook this mosque weeks ago. I thought I had gotten the last of them, but I guess there was one left. And he got to your friends."

"They weren't my friends; I was just driving their van. I'm not a homo—"

"Listen, you goddamned homophobe, I'm telling you, they were zombies."

"Oh, okay, bro. I'm just saying, anyway."

"Help me drag these bodies out of the masjid."

They made a pile of corpses in the mosque's parking lot, where Basim took a can of gas from the back of his desert-worn jeep and set them ablaze. "Let's get out of here so we don't have to smell them," said Basim.

Even though the members of Zulfikar would not live to see the ultimate battle between al-Mahdi and al-Dajjal, they'd still given their lives on the path of struggle, and there'd be no reason for them not to be counted among the martyrs. Back in Buffalo, Ayyub had a book called *The Spectacle of Death* that went into all of the hadiths and various traditions describing rewards and punishments in the afterlife. He tried to remember some of the things it said about paradise, besides talking about the houris, but his brain was in no shape to do anything, running as it was on speed and Stacker 2 and no sleep, and leaving behind the horrible bloodshed of zombies and Shiite death-metal stars. Ayyub looked at Basim, driving them through the Utah desert. Basim's eyes were on the road (though soon there was no road at all, only a never-ending wasteland of salt), his right hand relaxed but still strong on the wheel, and the left resting slack on his vinyl thigh. For a second Ayyub saw the Jehangir in him. The doomed punk-saint Jehangir had lived like a '77 Oi! whiskey rebel and found his Karbala in a mosh pit, but Basim was his living manifestation in the goth scene. Basim moved with Jehangir's irresistible physical charisma (which distinguished him from sidekicks like Amazing Ayyub, who could only scamper and scurry across the land like mad little rats) and lived with Jehangir's compassionate carelessness, which might end up redeeming the world by accident; Ayyub could see Basim falling drunk off a bridge into a freezing river below, only to have his body plug a huge crack in the dam and save the town. Basim's eventual martyrdom, however it went down, would someday cause the federal government to put his face on a postage stamp, mohawk and all, and American public schools would close on his 'urs (death anniversary) while he was up in Paradise with the eternally renewing virgins. Jehangir and Basim— those kinds of boys were made only to be slaughtered. They knew and accepted it, and sometimes they hurt for knowing, but deep down they loved their role.

"You know who your face looks like?" asked Amazing Ayyub.

"Who?" asked Basim, turning casually to look at Ayyub, since there was nothing in the desert for his jeep to hit.

"That fucker in that band . . . what was their name?"

"My Chemical Romance?"

"Yeah, you look like that fucker."

"I get that a lot," said Basim.

"You look like him."

"Okay." And Basim's eyeliner was sunna. Prophet Muhammad wore eyeliner, he'd tell Amazing Ayyub; they called it surmah or kohl.

Basim drove them deeper into the sand flats than anyone could ever have gone, far past the farthest I love Jennifer written in stones, past the point at which the world became only white salt and blue sky with no gas stations, no highway signs, no tracks from anything but the jeep, no life except theirs, the noplace-place where riding a jeep across the desert with a shotgun-toting goth put you in a new kind of Musa madness filled with harsh lawgiver prophets and dune-buggy legions primed for the eschatology to turn real, for the jealous god who hears bismillah before you slit a chicken's neck to bring it down. Khwajah Ahmad Yasavi said to imagine the world as a green dome in which there was nothing but Allah and you, and remember Allah until al-tajalli al-qahri overcame you and freed you from yourself until nothing remained but Allah, and Amazing Ayyub wasn't sure where he had heard that and he didn't remember the name Khwajah Ahmad Yasavi and he had no idea what al-tajalli al-qahri meant, but still he thought he was doing it.

Basim's campsite consisted of a green army tent, a large unknown item covered in blue tarp, and a wrapped body on a funeral pyre.

"Who's that?" asked Amazing Ayyub.

"Shahjehan," Basim answered. "They got him, they got Shahjehan."

"No fucking way!" spit Ayyub. "I thought you'd go first."

"Say ar-Rahman before you burn him!" called the gruff voice of an old black man from inside the tent. He climbed out, stroking his tufty gray fistful of holy-man beard, and hunched over. "Say the whole sura—it'll make a burning corpse smell like Ethiopian musk."

"Wolfman," said Basim, "this is Amazing Ayyub."

"As-salamu alaikum, brother!" said the Wolfman.

"Wa alaikum as-salam," answered Ayyub. As they shared a hearty embrace, Ayyub felt bad about his road stench, wondering if maybe ar-Rahman would make him smell like Ethiopian musk, too.

"Wolfman's a professor at the Hakim Bey Diocesan Theological College," said Basim.

"For real?"

"A canonical erection of the Moorish Orthodox Church of New Jersey," the Wolfman explained, adding that Junayd of Baghdad said that "no one attains to the Degree of Truth until a thousand honest people have testified that he is a heretic."

"Right on," Amazing Ayyub replied.

"Wolfman's always giving knowledge out here," said Basim.

"They really got Shahjehan?" Amazing Ayyub asked, turning to face the surviving Komina. "What the fuck, bro?"

"Shahj was a good kid," said Basim. "He could have been somewhere else besides the desert with us."

"Nah."

"What'd you say?"

"He was meant for out here," said Ayyub. "Doesn't matter if he was boys with Musharraf's kid or Junoon or any of those fuckers—he didn't fit in there."

"Yeah, Shahj looked like an engineer, but he was more punk than any of us."

"The Kominas were good shit, bro, A-plus."

"Thanks, Amazing Ayyub."

"Reminds me of watching rainbows with my buddy," he said with a snort-laugh.

"What's up with Rabeya?" asked Basim.

"I think she killed Matt Damon, but I don't know."

"The Kominas had a song named 'Rabeya,' but it was named after a different girl."

"Rabeya gave me the chills," said Ayyub. "I always felt like she saw through me, right to the fuckin' bone."

"You ever listen to Bauhaus?"

"What's that?"

"You don't know Bauhaus?"

"Nah, man."

"Bauhaus," said Basim, "the founders of goth. Peter Murphy got really into Sufism and moved to Turkey."

"Goth fags," said Ayyub.

"Amazing Ayyub, I'll fight you."

"All right, then."

Basim grabbed at Amazing Ayyub's arms, and they tumbled to the ground, Ayyub on his back and Basim on top,

Ayyub with his legs wrapped tight, Royce Gracie–style, around Basim's waist, squeezing hard. Basim gave Ayyub an accidental head butt, and a drop of Basim-sweat fell and stung Ayyub's eye. Ayyub then planted his right foot into the salt, kicked off with his left, and flipped them. Now on top, belly to belly, Ayyub tried manipulating Basim's arms into some kind of lock, but Basim squirmed until he found himself on his stomach, Ayyub still on top and breathing hard into his ear. Ayyub tucked his right forearm under Basim's chin and with a left hand full of hair shoved the back of Basim's head. Basim got air by squeezing an arm between his neck and Ayyub's arm. Then he put both hands on the back of Ayyub's head and wrenched down with full strength, forcing Ayyub to tap out.

Both men released their grips and rolled away from each other, the shared tangle of arms and legs once again becoming two men. Ayyub stayed for a long time on his back, arms and legs outstretched, Basim next to him on his stomach, both men breathing hard.

"You're going to kill them," said Basim.

"Who?"

"Shah 79. You're going to take those devils off the planet."

"Probably," Ayyub shrugged. Basim pulled himself up and tried to brush the salt off his latex chest. Some of the paint had smeared onto Ayyub. The Amazing One sat up, and Basim wiped the salt off his opponent's back.

"You have to, Amazing Ayyub. Somebody has to."

"Yeah, bro."

"Well, I've got something for you." Basim walked over to whatever it was he covered with that blue tarp and whipped off the tarp to reveal an AK-47, like the one Rabeya had pointed at Matt Damon but freakishly large—maybe the size of a small motorcycle, with a cartoonishly disproportionate banana clip longer than Ayyub's leg.

"How am I gonna get this to Buffalo?" Ayyub asked, his voice cracking. "What am I gonna do, bring it on a bus?"

"That's easy," said Basim. "You recite Ya Sin."

"Ya Sin. *Ya Sin?* I recite fuckin' Ya Sin?"

"You say it with the right niyya, Ya Sin becomes an invisibility spell."

"Horseshit."

"Do you know the sura? Here, hold on." Basim walked over to his tent, stuck his head in, fished around, and came out with a thin para. "Get your niyya straight and read it." Facing the gun, as though it were the mihrab in a mosque or a body to be prayed over, Ayyub opened the para to its first page. It had been a long time since he'd read the Qur'an, but he hadn't forgotten how, and he could start easily enough: Aoudhu billahi mina shaytani rajeem, bismillahir Rahmanir Raheem—Yaaaaaa Seeeeeeen . . . after that it got harder, but Ayyub plodded through: WalQur'anil hakim, innaka laminal mursaleen, ala siratin mustaqeem, tanzeela alzeezir-raheem, litunzira qaman ma unthira aba uhum fahum ghafiloon, laqad haqqa alqawul ala aktharihim fahum la yuminoon, inna ja'alna fi anaqihim aghlalan fahiya illa al-athqani fahum muqmahoon, waja alna min bayni aydihim saddan wamin khalfihim saddan faaghshaynahum fahum la yubsiroon, wasawaun alayhim anthartahum am lam tunthirhum am lam tunthirhum la yuminoon, innama tunthiru mani itabaa alththikra wakhashiya alrahmana bilghaybi fabashshirhu bimaghfiratin waajrin kareem, inna nahnu nuhyee almawta wanaktubu ma qaddamoo waatharahum wakulla shay'in ahsaynahu fee imamin mubeen, waidrib lahum mathalan as-haba alqaryati ith jaaha almursaloon, ith arsalna ilayhimu ithnayni fakaththaboohuma fa'azazna bithalithin faqaloo inna ilaykum mursaloon, qaloo ma antum illa basharun mithluna wama anzala ar-rahmanu min shay'in in antum illa takthiboon, qaloo rabbuna ya'alamu inna ilaykum lamursaloon, wama alayna illa albalaghu almubeen . . .

"You're gone," gasped the Komina.

"I'm gone? I'm not even at the twentieth ayat."

"Yeah, but you're fucking vanished, Ayyub. Keep reading— read the whole thing."

Later that night, Amazing Ayyub was still invisible and Shahjehan's body was burning on the pyre. Basim's reading of ar-Rahman made Ethiopian-musk smoke. Invisible Ayyub, Basim, and the Wolfman sat by the fire in Basim's lawn chairs, drinking beer and telling stories. Basim had to back up his chair because the fire was melting his latex shirt. They told stories about girls and Islam. Basim thought it was funny to be hanging out in the desert with a guy called the Wolfman and shooting zombies as if they lived in a B movie, *Zombies vs. Wolfman and the Muslim Punk Rockers*.

"Clearly, Islam is one," writes Tariq Ramadan in *Western*

Muslims and the Future of Islam, and "presents a body of opinion whose essential axes are identifiable and accepted by the various trends or schools of thought . . ." Invisible Amazing Ayyub, melted-latex Basim Usmani, and the scraggly Wolfman wouldn't have known if they represented a new school of thought out there in the salt flats, and Tariq Ramadan wasn't around to provide a scholarly insight, but Tariq Ramadan had nothing to say to those guys, so fuck him.

Malcolm X's grandson had told me to go read *God's Unruly Friends,* by Ahmet Karamustafa, which described medieval Sufi groups that "real" Islam has swept under the rug: butt-balling Qalandars, genital-piercing Haydaris, boozing and self-lacerating Jamis, and the Madaris of northern India, who had long, matted hair, rejected rituals, smoked hashish all day, and rubbed their naked bodies with the ashes. Karamustafa suggested that orthodox Islam had spread as the product of an Arab cultural elite, only to be undone by the conversion of isolated and non-Arabic-speaking peoples: lower-caste Hindus, Turkish nomads, and sub-Saharan Africans. Left out on Islam's geographic, economic, and linguistic fringes, cut off from the big universities, they could only be Muslims of their own design.

It also happened in the wilderness of North America, where Islam took new forms—irrefutably black, with its own black scriptures, black symbols and black holy men—that the immigrant kids from Pakistan would never get. This black Islam even spawned strange white culture seeds; from the Moorish Science Temple came the Moorish Orthodox Church, with opium-waltzing Walid al-Taha and his student Hakim Bey using "the black man's code to fit their facts," as Norman Mailer said of the Kerouacs and Ginsbergs. Many these days would also view the Progressive Islam scene as a homegrown heresy, and American Muslim women have fired the first shots to create a whole other Islam for themselves. And now even the bums and punks are starting to stand up on the margins—kids like the Kominas' Basim and dead zombie Shahjehan—to claim their corner.

Basim's own Islam was a cultural thing, and being a fellow immigrant's son, Amazing Ayyub related to that Islam on a level that I couldn't with my convert experience—for the converts, Islam is only books; there's no heart or culture or family tenderness, which is why we often go nuts. The Wolfman couldn't relate to the immigrant Sunnism either, being an ancient convert from the First Resurrection, so he listened while Basim and Ayyub shared stories. When he lived in Pakistan, Basim took part in the national sport of kite fighting, in which kids coated their kite strings with broken glass and had dogfights in the sky. Basim had a scar on his throat from the time a rival's string almost took his head off.

"Where's your family from?" Basim asked Invisible Ayyub, turning to face him even though he couldn't see the punk.

"Iran," Ayyub answered. "We're Persian." It was hard for Basim, and maybe the Wolfman, to even imagine Ayyub—

legendary Amazing Ayyub, the scourge of adult-video stores, Ayyub who got hand jobs at homeless shelters, slept in abandoned cars, and wandered the earth with no one to love him— ever having a family or coming from somewhere.

"You know about al-Hallaj?" asked the Wolfman. "He was Persian."

"Yeah, they fucked him up," Ayyub replied. "They fucked him like a champ."

"He danced and laughed all the way to his execution," interjected Basim, with secret dreams of someday dancing to his own.

"They gave him a thousand lashes," added the Wolfman. "They cut off his hands and feet, hung him until the morning, and then decapitated him. But do you know why?"

"He said he was al-Haqq," Ayyub answered. "That's a name of God; you can't fuck around with that."

"Naw, man, that's not why they did it. Read your Ernst, man!"

"Hallaj said he was al-Haqq."

"Yeah, but that's not why they killed him. They killed Hallaj because he said you could make the pilgrimage anywhere you wanted and perform the rites in your own backyard and it counts the same as a hajj to Mecca."

"No shit?"

"No shit, brother."

Out of the three men, only the Wolfman had been to the real Mecca. He was only seven years old, he told them, with a daddy fresh out of Elijah's Nation, following in the footsteps of Malik Shabazz . . . The Wolfman told Basim and Ayyub how on the plane, he thought all of the Arabic being spoken around him was Qur'an. What he remembered most was the birds, the Baytullah Pigeons, who flew all over the Masjid Haram but wouldn't fly directly over the Kaaba for anything. Wolfman drew in the air to demonstrate their movements: Say they'll be flying this way, and they're headed toward the Kaaba—they'll make a sharp turn right out of its way, and if they're going *this* way, then right before going over the Kaaba, they turn *that* way and go around and then go back on their right direction . . . and they won't sit on it, the way birds like to perch on things.

When birds sing or dogs bark or anything like that, the Wolfman told them, it's what they call a zikr, you know? They're saying *Allah*, that's all.

Later, Basim brought out sleeping bags and mugs of bhang lassi, lassi made with cannabis leaves. They slept by the Ethiopian musk–smelling fire of Shahjehan's cremation, the first time Amazing Ayyub ever fell asleep invisible. Basim kept his shotgun close by in case any zombies showed up. "Sleep with the remembrance of death," said somebody named Uwais al-Qami, "and rise with the awareness that you will not live long."

In the morning, the Wolfman gave Ayyub a pouch of salt (straight from the ground they walked on) and specific instructions for how to use it when courting jinns in a cemetery. "That's where jinns like to hang out," said the Wolfman. "Cemeteries, toilets, those kinds of places, you know. And they like holes in the ground; there was this one hadith from Qatadah, he said that 'Abdullah ibn Sarjas said that the Prophet forbade you from pissing into a hole. Qatadah asked ibn Sarjas why the Prophet said that, and he told him that the jinns lived in there."

"Jinns sound like punks," Ayyub replied. "The Prophet would have been all right by us."

"They got their own scene," Basim interrupted. "They call it jinncore. It's kind of like psychobilly. They have their own labels and put on shows. Bands like the Bidah Billyz, Zombie Rockets, Black Jinn Curse, the Jinn City Rockers, and some other ones."

The Wolfman told Amazing Ayyub that there were three types of jinns. The first type had wings and flew around, the second looked like snakes and dogs, and the third would stop for a rest before resuming its journey. He'd gotten that information from a hadith narrated by Abu Tha'labah al-Khushani.

"Are there, like, girl jinns?" Ayyub asked.

"Oh, sure," said the Wolfman, laughing. "They got some girl jinns. I don't know what you want with them, but they got 'em."

Amazing Ayyub picked up his massive gun, which became invisible at his touch, gave salam to his friends, and went off on his way.

For a long time, I just had Amazing Ayyub walking by himself, which in a place like the desert makes you feel like you're living out a movie. Walking alone gave the new assassin time to reflect on his mission and build up some fantasies in his head of how it'd go down, until he went far enough into it that Shah 79, as his victims, were bigger than Shah 79 could ever be, since the act of murder began to feel like a psychic healing: Shah 79 was no longer Shah 79 — Shah 79 was now an Eid goat.

When he saw a lone figure coming toward him in the distance, Amazing Ayyub's first thought was *zombie*. He readied his gun. Then he remembered that he was invisible, and chances were that the zombie wouldn't even know he was there. They'd pass each other without issue, Ayyub thought, like two ships in the night.

Then the figure was close enough to take on some definition, and Amazing Ayyub could see that it didn't walk like a zombie, that it was a Caucasian male in his early to mid-twenties, with a vaguely nerdy indie-rock sensibility, sporting an electric guitar hanging from his shoulder by a wide leather strap.

"AS-SALAMS SALAIKUM!" he shouted, waving his arms while the guitar dangled.

"YOU CAN'T SEE ME!" screamed Amazing Ayyub. "I'M INVISIBLE!"

"I CAN SEE YOU!"

"He must be a fucking jinn or somethin'," Ayyub muttered. The guy started half running toward him. Ayyub stayed at his walking pace.

"You're Amazing Ayyub! As-salams salaikum." He had fucked up the "salams," but Ayyub didn't notice.

"Wa alaikum as-salam." They shook hands.

"You're Amazing Ayyub!"

"Yeah?"

"You have no idea what it means for me to find you out here! You're the new American Islam; you're the looming paradigm shift! It's all on you, Amazing Ayyub—you're what needs to be studied! You're the dialogue between civilizations! What are you doing, man? You should have professors following you around out here!"

"Are you a professor?"

"I'm a TA. I'm getting my PhD in Islamic Studies."

"What'd you do, convert? Or—"

"No, I'm not actually Muslim. I call myself a progressive spiritual agnostic."

"What the fuck you doing, then?"

"Amazing Ayyub, I'm totally cool. I mean, I'm not some koofar just appropriating your culture—I get it; I'm dead on. I consume Ghazali all day, and my analysis is completely out of hand, off the chart. I know my shit. You don't even know who you're talking to."

"Whatever, bro."

"Amazing Ayyub, I'm so endlessly *fascinated* with what's going on in the community in this country—you know, the Progressive movement, women-led prayer. It's so amazing, Muslim women reclaiming the rights that Prophet Muhammad, peace be upon him, gave them in the seventh century. Did you go to the woman-led salaatul-jum'aa in New York, the Amina Wadud prayer?"

"No," shrugged Ayyub. "What if I got a boner lookin' at her sujdah?"

"I went, and I found it so . . . *fascinating*."

"What'd you go for if you're not Muslim?"

"I was observing, you know, and I just wanted to show my support. I was in the back and didn't interfere or anything. I just—"

"Who cares if you support it or not if you're not even Muslim?"

"Right, right, absolutely. But I did want to talk to some people there and learn about some of the interpretations behind it—you know, what it says in the Ko-ran about this sort of thing . . ."

"What's with the guitar?"

"Amazing Ayyub, I want to be your herald."

"What's that mean?"

"You need someone to herald your arrival. There's a lot about you that could be misunderstood, and you need someone with the right kind of training and academic background to put you in proper context."

"I have a proper context?"

"Well, as the 'awaam—"

"The what?"

"The 'awaam, the general Muslim population. The 'awaam have a certain kind of truth, enjoyed at their own level of understanding . . . but you can't really implement that truth without instruction and guidance from the khawaas. It's the khawaas who offer analysis from a level that the 'awaam are unable or unwilling to—"

"So, you're the what, now?"

"The khawaas, the intellectual leaders of the Muslim community."

"You're not Muslim, though."

"But I'm part of the conversation, right? Within the academic—but anyway, I'm trying to help you. You ever read Farid Esack?"

"Who?"

"These social-justice elements of Islam just blow my mind. Ayyub, we need to show how you're more than a grubby, idol-smashing punk rocker; you're not just iconoclastic for iconoclasm's sake—you really do engage the traditions. The Progressive Muslim scholars today aren't having a proper discourse with the marginalized . . . and *you're* the marginalized; you're the one they need to understand. We need someone young and cool to really capture the truth of what you're doing, and I think that I'm the one." The man nodded to his guitar. "And then there are certain legalistic issues we have to work through—you know, people would want to make takfir on you and such, and I've been doing quite a bit of reading on this sort of thing. We're going to find a place for you within the legislation, a whole new Western Progressive Fiqh, maybe. Can you imagine it? You'd be surprised, but there really is a place and a precedent for you in the greater history of Islam. You're the heir to a whole preexisting . . . I mean, the taqwacores are like modern-day Qalandars, don't you think?"

"What the fuck's a Qalandar?"

So, as Amazing Ayyub's new herald, the PhD student

walked about ten feet in front of him, riffing away on his guitar as though a cheering crowd awaited them on the edge of the salt flats.

"Did I tell you I'm working on a novel?"

"What's your novel about?" asked Ayyub.

"A PhD student."

Amazing Ayyub just trudged along and stayed inside his own head while the kid kept rambling, using words that Ayyub didn't know. It wasn't clear if the PhD student just assumed that Ayyub comprehended his language or if he was only trying to put himself over, but either way, Ayyub didn't know what "exegesis" meant, he didn't know what "ontological" or "metanarrative" meant, and he didn't know what a "moral nexus" was. This asshole kept on grinding Ayyub's nerves until Ayyub had no problem shooting his herald in the back and leaving his body for the zombies. Ayyub moved on without a qualified expert to announce his emergence into the world.

I wrote stories that put me in Buffalo, but really I was in Massachusetts; on my way back from an "Islamic Anarchism" panel at some conference in D.C., I stopped in Lowell to ride around with the Kominas (Basim was showing me Boston and rambling about its distinctly Irish punk scene, and he said, "Sorry, man, I've got a fetish for your culture," to which I replied, "It's okay, I've got one for yours") and decided that I'd just stay there and live in my green 1997 Buick Skylark. With the backseat down, I had managed to construct a lumpy but acceptable bed and could stretch out with my feet in the trunk. In Lowell, I was always tired enough to sleep hard. I had my weights with me, ate only canned tuna, and was starting to feel like an Amazing Ayyub in my own right: skinny but ripped, with round delts, expanding lats, and veins popping out of my forearms. Like Ayyub, I smelled horrible but carried myself with full confidence. Spent most of my time with the Kominas and this Indian kid Hasan, who kept calling me his "nigga." Look, I told him, first off, I'm the son of a white supremacist— you don't know what kind of purging I do; second, I build with the Five Percenters and couldn't ever let it get back to them that I allow such talk in my cipher; and third, Hasan, you're a desi going into law school, a maid comes to clean your parents' house, and you live whiter than me. You have no business ever saying the word, even if you're trying to be ironic about it. Not sure that he understood; his Naseeb.com profile declared him something like "Hasan Da Bomb," and he'd use that to mack online with little Muslim sisters.

Usually I parked my car across the street from one of the UMass Lowell campuses or by the neighboring Hess station. I couldn't lock my car from the outside, because it wouldn't unlock, but when I was inside, I could lock it and the Skylark turned into a bunker. I could poke my head up and survey the parking lot, almost believing that none of the cigarette-breaking Hess clerks or pretty college girls or whoever could even see me.

In Boston I knew a Muslim girl who wore hijab—not the

sheer and sparkly Club ISNA hijab, but a solid and sturdy cotton wrap that framed the face tight for a sister standing firm on her square, legit in her deen. We got to talking about boys and girls and relationships, and of course I told her that I perceived females as a sad sacrifice of my lifestyle.

"Girls can't live the way I live," I said.

"You haven't met the right girl," she replied.

"I haven't met a girl who could last a night in my car."

She laughed that off and said that she could and would sleep in my car, no problem, so we drove around looking for a place more private than the Hess parking lot and found a rest stop on the road to New Hampshire. We crawled onto my makeshift bed and shared the blankets. I had my arm underneath her and before long, we got to the first kiss. When we finally worked our way to the Muslim Girl Hand Job, my second or third shot made a high arc and hit her on the top of her head, right on the hijab. We both laughed about it.

The next night I left my car in Lowell, and future zombie fodder Shahjehan took me to an uneventful party full of UMass theater assholes. He dropped me off in the morning, and I climbed into the back of my car to sleep. Soon I noticed that I had more room to move my legs; my weights were gone. I jumped out and looked around like the guy might still be there. Who'd rob a car that looked like mine? And who runs down the street carrying two hundred pounds of weights? I tried to remember what else was in the car that could have been worth taking. The ashtray was still filled with my toll change, but the thief had taken the red backpack containing my digital camera (a Christmas present from Mom) and three or four notebooks filled with the handwritten Amazing Ayyub Masoom story.

The story was the story, maybe not completely cohesive or following a straight narrative path so much as it was big chunks of action and scenery and notes on how the characters should talk and look, and what kinds of things ought to be captured about them. I had written about Amazing Ayyub vowing to kill the Muslim pop-punk band Shah 79 and originally planned to base it on my own failed mission to assassinate Reel Big Fish with a Super Soaker at Fredonia College in 2002. I was there for the big "Fredfest" with my friends, hanging out in my luchador mask with the Super Soaker loaded, ready to take those devils off the planet, and the assholes walked right past us! I even said, "What up" to one of them, and then Pete told me, "Dude, that was them, that was Reel Big Fish." As it turned out, I make a lousy assassin.

In the notebooks I also confessed a growing, perverted fondness for Abu Musab Al-Zarqawi, the Jordanian who assumed Osama bin Laden's role as head of Al-Qaeda. I imagined Amazing Ayyub reading his biography through repeated trips to Barnes & Noble, where he'd keep dog-earing pages on the same copy to save his place. "Zarqawi does not intend to make a career," writes Jean-Charles Brisard. "What he is trying to do is take revenge on life." Ayyub might have gotten into this guy, too, at least until the part where it's shown that Zarqawi hates Shi'as.

Born Ahmad Fadil, Zarqawi was expelled from Al-Zarqa High School, dropped out, made lots of visits to the Ma'soum cemetery, played soccer on the back streets, picked his share of fights, got a job at the paper factory, lost it after six months, served his required two years in the military, came home, and put so many tattoos on his arms that people called him the Green Man. He caught some busts for shoplifting, drug dealing, and a stabbing, after which Mom tried to turn her son around by putting him in religious school. At the mosque, he lucked into a shot at seeing the world and having adventures: the Afghan jihad. Ahmad first arrived in Peshawar and crossed over into Afghanistan just as the Soviets were withdrawing, but he chose to stick around anyway, bonding with a hospitalized fighter who had lost his leg to a land mine, hanging out with warlords, joining the civil war on the side of the Pashtun.

In 1992 he made hajj to Mecca, first asking an imam back home to pray that Allah might "forget him a little." Upon his return, he opened a video-rental store, which went out of business, and spent most of his time at the mosque, where his inflated war stories made him a big shot to the unemployed local boys. He renamed himself Musab—after Musab Ben Umayr, the Prophet's companion who lost both his hands in jihad—with the surname Zarqawi, to make his hometown proud. The story does have some charm; if Zarqawi had been a Boston skin who took off to Belfast and joined the IRA, he could have become the working-class hero of a Dropkick Murphys pub anthem.

When the cops came for him, Zarqawi had a submachine gun with three rounds and thirty-five cartridges but gave up without a fight. In prison he memorized the Qur'an, built his own weights from pieces of his bed and olive oil cans filled with stones, told tall tales of Afghanistan, and refused to wear the prison's required uniform. After his release he stayed with relatives for a while, made halfhearted attempts to find a job, considered buying a truck to sell fruit on the street, and eventually went back to Pakistan. He landed himself in prison in both Pakistan and Iran, and in Kandahar, Afghanistan, pulled himself out of the rubble after an American missile strike.

"He was a sort of hoodlum in the city of Zarqa," Jordan's King Abdullah would say after Zarqawi attained Al-Qaeda superstardom. "He did not have the reputation of being an intelligent or brilliant man. All of a sudden, when he was just a criminal and a drunk, he found himself in the nets of Al-Qaeda." I get him; he's more a personality type than a product of a specific value system. Zarqawi started out as a street punk and became a religious extremist. The flip isn't so drastic as it sounds; I've made it, too, but the other way around.

I wondered how my stolen notebooks looked to their new owner. The digital camera had only a few pictures on it, but they were lost moments and specific collections of people that could never again be achieved: scenes from the weekend of the Amina Wadud prayer in New York, assortments of friends from all over the place, and Progressive

Muslim stars who aren't even on speaking terms now. The more I thought about it, the more it made sense to wonder if Allah Subhanahu wa ta'Ala was kicking my ass for getting hand jobs from sweet Muslim girls. You can't ejaculate on someone's hijab without expecting some kind of cosmic ramification—it could be as bad a form of blasphemy as anything.

Either way, Allah willed that the Amazing Ayyub stuff had to be rewritten. It might have been a mercy. Maybe those original notebooks contained an idea so heretical and spiritually dangerous that it couldn't make its way to a finished manuscript, lest I destroy myself and anyone else who latched on to its ignorance.

AMAZING AYYUB VS.

THE
PSYCHOBILLY JINNS

MICHAEL MUHAMMAD KNIGHT drove to the liquor store (the one on Grant Street with the white wooden horse) so he could cash a check, and heard the news that on Herkimer Street that morning, a woman had been found partially cannibalized. The author worried about Amazing Ayyub, should he ever come home, and then bought one of those insane vinegar-sausage sticks in an unnaturally bright shade of red, the ones Ayyub used to call "Ashura for your intestines." The author took his money and his sausage and sat on the curb by the Zul-Jannah. Everyone walking past him into the liquor store looked beaten up and sad.

Amazing Ayyub was using his Ya Sin invisibility spell to hitch rides on flatbed trailers, going hundreds of miles at a stretch, holding on for his life. Out there in the open air at upwards of 100 miles per hour, the wind did a terrible number on his skin, dried him right out. Whenever the coked-out trucker stopped to fuel up or rest, Amazing Ayyub would jump off, recuperate, and wait around for another one. Sometimes he turned visible in hopes of socializing at truck stops, but it never went anywhere, and he always ended up cloaking himself again.

By the will of Allah alone, Amazing Ayyub ended up in Oklahoma City, where journeyman scenester Al Rukn happened to be lording over a taqwacore house. Al was a half-black, half-Emirati kid who'd come up in New York hardcore, found Sufism in his late teens, and made for a mean, drunk Jerrahi. Amazing Ayyub found a pay phone and told Al where he was.

Al Rukn came by in a beat-up blue Chevy Celebrity, the rear covered in taqwacore band stickers. They put Amazing Ayyub's machine gun in the back but had to leave the trunk open for it to fit.

"The taqwacores are coming together in Oklahoma," said Al as he drove. "It's slow, but we're building."

"You got a lot of Muslim punks out here?" asked Ayyub.

"Not Muslim punks," Al replied. "Taqwacores. We don't say 'Muslim punk' around here because, number one, some of this stuff is neither Muslim nor punk, and number two, have you ever seen *Afropunk*?"

"What's that?"

"It was a whole documentary about these black punk-rock kids, but my point is that the film gets into an identity game that we're not playing. We're not into the whole 'minority displaced within another disenfranchised subculture' angle; that's not how we define ourselves. We've got our own separate scene."

"That's A-plus, Al Rukn."

"How are the Kominas?"

"The zombies killed Shahjehan."

"Shahjehan? Are you sure?"

"They got him, bro."

"*Fuck!*" Al Rukn punched his tacky blue steering wheel.

"Basim cremated him so he wouldn't turn into a zombie."

"Well, I guess that was the right thing to do. Shahjehan was a good kid. He had his heart in the right place. We're all fuckups and we have no problem with it, but Shahj, Shahj honestly believed that he was doing right by Islam. Where the shit are the zombies coming from?"

"Fuck if I know," answered Amazing Ayyub, "but Basim was killing the shit out of them. You shoulda seen him; he was like, *Blam blam blam!*"

"There'll be more."

Al Rukn brought Ayyub to the littered lawn and crumbling porch of his taqwacore house and parked his car on the dead grass. Ayyub could hear a three-piece taqwa band in melodic but thrashing rehearsal, coming through the walls to greet them.

"Who's that?"

"My housemates. It's kind of poppy and skater, but they're good for what they do." Al and Ayyub walked into the house, and Ayyub saw them right there, filling the living room with amps and assorted cords: three skinny Malay kids with spiked and dyed hair. He maneuvered past them without introductions or even a nod, heading for the couch as though pulled to it by a magnet. The couch was Ayyub's natural habitat—not any couch in particular, but every couch in the world, regardless of its condition. This one looked like it had been found by a curb on garbage day and smelled like it had seen hard times, but did what it had to for a wayfaring bum. Ayyub sank into the beat-up cushions and murdered springs, propped his big gun against the couch, and watched the band play in front of him. Al Rukn ventured elsewhere in the house to get a beer, came back with two bottles, and gave Ayyub one. He took a seat next to Ayyub's gun and reached around it to shout in Ayyub's ear, trying to be heard above the song but still taking refuge in its shroud of noise: "THE DRUMMER'S GOT A SISTER, AMAZING AYYUB . . ."

"IS SHE HERE?"

"NO, SHE'S NOT HERE . . . BUT SHE'S A CUTE LIL' MALAY GIRL IN TRIANGLE HIJAB AND RAMONES T-SHIRTS. BRO, YOU HAVE NO IDEA, BUT I CAN'T GET NEAR HER . . ."

"THAT SUCKS," Ayyub shouted back.

"AL-HAMDULILLAH," answered Al Rukn. "THE GIRL'S JUST TOO PRISTINE; THERE'S THAT

SWEETNESS ABOUT HER, YOU KNOW? TO TRY AND TAMPER WITH HER IS LIKE AN ANTI-ISLAMIC ACT—I REALLY BELIEVE THAT."

The song concluded, the room became quiet again, and Al Rukn sealed the shared secret with a knowing look at Ayyub. "Hey, guys," he said to the Malay kids, "this here is Amazing Ayyub, with authenticity beyond anyone's comprehension." Ayyub shared salams with each of them. "C'mon Ayyub," said Al. "I've got some shit you need to see." They went upstairs to Al's room, a clusterfuck of film equipment, recording equipment, wires and cords, tall stacks and less orderly piles of CDs, and a heavy-duty untopped tripod that could have supported either a large camera or a Gatlin gun.

Al Rukn sat before his computer, moved some CDs, a stack of papers, and a .38 snub-nosed revolver out of the way, and pushed his mouse around.

"Amazing Ayyub, you want to see the real shit?"

"Fuckin' A," Ayyub replied. Vulgarities peppered taqwacore dialogues to the point of either becoming meaningless, like those constant mash'Allahs, insha'Allahs, and subhana'Allahs in conversations of the pious, or effortlessly replacing actual vocabulary, like the word "smurf" in Smurf-speak. Al Rukn clicked off the songs, opened an mpeg, and set the window to full screen. First it was all black, and they heard Shahjehan's electric-guitar adhan; then the screen faded into the white wilderness of Utah. "That's the salt flats," Ayyub remarked. "You see all that shit? It looks like snow on the ground, right? It's not, though—it's salt. Oh, damn, that's Basim . . ."

The accompanying soundtrack turned to the Kominas' "Shariah Law in the USA," with Basim wailing, *I am an Islamist, I am an antichrist* . . .

Al Rukn and Amazing Ayyub watched Basim, with his latex-paint shirt and flimsy mohawk, shotgun in hand, staring down a zombie tied to a post. The zombie let out a brainless groan.

"Watch this," said Al. "Watch this zombie's head."

Basim pumped his sawed-off and took aim. Al turned up his computer's speakers. Ayyub jumped at the shot. *Jesus!*

Then they watched doomed Shahjehan Khan premartyrdom, shahadah bandanna wrapped around his forehead, running the Kominas' makeshift obstacle course: crawling on his stomach under coils of razor wire, swinging from ropes, hopping tires on the ground like a high school football player, pole-vaulting over fences, attacking burlap-bag zombie dummies with machetes and hatchets, then tossing live grenades at the horizon while Arabic text occupied the bottom of the screen. "What is this?" Ayyub asked.

"The world's first zombie-slayer jihadi training video," Al answered.

"Fuckin' Shahj, look at him."

"He's a shaheed," said Al Rukn. "He went out the right way."

"You know about the houris?" asked Amazing Ayyub, but of course Al did; everyone knew about the seventy-two virgins in paradise, even non-Muslims. Talking heads on Fox News made the houris appear as essential a component of Islam as belief in tawhid. Al ignored the question and kept his eyes to the screen as he played with the mouse, clicking into files and seeing what else he had. "After you pop a houri," Ayyub continued, "she's automatically a virgin again. It just keeps growing back."

"Yeah, I heard about that," said Al. They kept drinking and building on the issue of zombies and the sad story of Shahjehan Khan. Later, both chemically destroyed and walking the streets—Amazing Ayyub carrying his big gun and waiting for a squirrel to shoot, Al Rukn telling crazy drunk stories, Amazing Ayyub adding an occasional "No way!" and "Are you fuckin' serious?" to keep them going— the two plastered taqwacores found themselves at the front gate of a cemetery.

The Tenth Imam, Imam Ali al-Naqi, dug a grave beside his prayer rug and said, "In order to remember my end, I keep the grave before my eyes." He spent twelve years in jail before finally getting poisoned on orders of the Caliph al-Mu'taz. He's buried in holy Samarra, Iraq. Michael Muhammad Knight was once in a cemetery with a desi girl and noticed her taking timid little baby steps. He asked her what the issue was and she replied, "I'm sorry, but this is only the second time I've ever been in a cemetery." As a child, she'd been taught that female wailing bothered corpses.

"We need the jinns on our side to take out the zombies," said Ayyub, leading the way past the gate.

"What are you doing, Amazing Ayyub?"

"We're gonna summon up a jinn army."

"That's serious, man. You don't know that you want to do that."

"Jinn army, bro, and then the zombies can't stop us." Ayyub dropped his gun behind a tombstone, walked to an empty space, and poured the salt in a large circle around himself. "Al Rukn, man, get in here." Al joined him in the cipher and the two sat down, encircled by Utah salt.

"Now what?" asked Al Rukn.

"Fuck if I remember, I'm fractured right now."

"Yeah, me too, brother."

"Amazing Ayyub, you're King Shit."

"I *am* King Shit."

"You're doing what needs to be done, bro. You're going to wipe out Shah 79—that's the word in the cipher."

"What?"

"C'mon, Ayyub. I know that's why you've got that big-ass crazy gun and you're lugging it across the country."

"Yeah, I need to find those guys. At first I was just gonna head to Buffalo and straighten out the kids; you know, I was thinking because I'm older and I've been around, they might listen—"

"Not gonna happen, Ayyub. No offense, but Shah 79 aren't listening to a guy like you. That's not where their heads are."

"I hear you, bro."

"Just blow 'em up like they're zombies," said Al Rukn. "Ayyub, man, you have to look at the shit that's going on right now. They're killing taqwacore with Islamo-chic."

"What's that?"

"Islamo-chic, bro. Marxism's not the language of resistance anymore; you have to change with the times. Listen to these goofball white kids in kifeyyehs, telling all their little anarchist friends that now it's Islam versus capitalism, that the last line of defense against U.S. hegemony is a solid worldwide ummah. They answer the cruel meat industry with Islamic zabiha dictates, racism with Malcolm's hajj, the commodification of female bodies with hijab. As our government fucks up more and more in Muslim countries, you'll see a steadily developing stream of leftist Islamophile poseurs. And that's where Shah 79 comes in."

"What do they have to do with it?"

"Once people in the wrong places caught wind of Islamo-chic, they had to find a way to co-opt it and sap out all the meaning, drain it of the naive but sincere resistance it offered. So here comes your Muslim pop-punk."

"That was their plan?"

"Fuck, Ayyub, I'd bet it's even written down somewhere as the *Protocols of the Elders of Taqwacore*. They're taking over and fucking us."

"That's why we need the jinns, bro."

"The jinns aren't doing shit, Ayyub."

"You know what the jinns are made of?"

"What?"

"Smokeless fire, bro. Can you imagine that?"

"Sure, Ayyub."

"They have girl jinns, too."

"Yeah."

"Would you . . . you know what I mean?"

"Would I what?"

"I don't know."

"Jesus Christ, Amazing Ayyub! I've got Nadia Nyce in town, I don't have to think about getting with jinns." Nadia Nyce was the stage name used by more than one desi porn star.

"Yo, Al Rukn, who was that band?"

"What band?"

"Those Malaysian taqwacore kids back at your house."

"They're the Android Sufoids," said Al Rukn. "I named them. Android Sufoid, that's real. I can shoot lasers out of my eyes that'll burn holes through your nafs." They studied the grass in front of them, neither saying anything, Ayyub secretly wondering if Al Rukn was crazy, then returning to thoughts of girl jinns. "This is bullshit!" cried Al.

"Give it a minute," said Amazing Ayyub.

"We're sitting here in a salt circle, waiting for the jinn army to show up, and they're not going to show up, Amazing Ayyub, and Shahjehan Khan is just smoke in the air. What the fuck is going on? Can you tell me that? Dudes are on *Good Morning America* now, talking about the presence of Muslim zombies and what that means for our community or the war on terror or God knows what the shit they're talking about . . . but man, I don't know where I'm going with this. I just know that I'm drunk and sitting in a cemetery, and I think it's the wrong night for it. I've got Nadia

Nyce in town—why aren't I over there?" Al Rukn got up and stepped out of the salt cipher, stumbling off on his own way and leaving Amazing Ayyub to face the jinns alone.

Ayyub wondered if there was some du'a he could say to summon the smokeless-fire ones, then suspected that the Wolfman had taught him one and he'd forgotten it, but his niyya was pure enough anyway.

Then the jinn came.

They were unimpressive handfuls of men, walking past Ayyub with early-Elvis hair and cuffed jeans but somehow gothed out, a sensibility vaguely reminiscent of classic 1950s greasers wrung through a B-grade horror flick. Ayyub left his salt circle to follow them. Flanked by jinn scenesters on all sides, he caught snippets of their conversations, mostly talk of bands and previous shows. Some of the jinns had vampy she-jinns on their arms. Every so often, Ayyub spotted a jinn lugging a stand-up bass, and before long he heard music in the distance.

They were walking toward a stage occupied by a frantic band of psychobilly jinns, the lead singer gyrating like a zombie Elvis, the crowd filled with bopping jinncores. Looking at the giant banner behind the band, Amazing Ayyub deduced that it was the Dung Eaters. He stood on the outer fringe, taking it all in, and after a while sensed that he was being stared at. He turned and found a fishnet-wearing jinn-girl with pompadoured smokeless-fire bangs.

"I think I know you," she exclaimed. "What's your name?"

"Amazing Ayyub."

"Yes!" She excitedly slapped his forearm. "Amazing Ayyub! I saw you in one of Harun's zines."

"Yeah, I remember that."

"You're like a legend to the taqwacores."

"You serious?"

"Of course. Even the jinncores know you."

"I've seen some things."

"What kind of things?"

"I don't know," said Ayyub. "There's some crazy shit out there."

"You know," she whispered in his ear, "the Prophet said that every human has a jinn companion."

"Is that right?"

"Maybe I'm your qareen, Amazing Ayyub. Maybe I've been at your side the whole way."

"You think—" She put her smokeless-fire lips on him, and he forgot what he wanted to say. They made out and he put his muddy hands in her shirt. Before long she unbuttoned him, spit on her smokeless-fire palm, and shoved it down his pants.

"What kinds of things have you seen, Amazing Ayyub?"

"I've seen all sorts of things, but I can't remember them now . . ."

"Were you in the desert?" She took a tighter grip and moved her whole body in rhythm with her hand.

"Yeah . . . yeah, I was in Utah . . ."

"Tell me about Utah, Amazing Ayyub. Did you see any taqwacores?"

"Probably so . . ."

"Did you see the Kominas?"

"How'd you . . . what?"

"DID YOU SEE THE KOMINAS OUT THERE, AMAZING AYYUB?" She jerked so hard it hurt him. "TALK TO ME, AMAZING AYYUB!" She kept her eyes locked on his and now had both hands in his pants, one jerking and the other playing with his balls like a stress toy. "WHAT WERE THE KOMINAS DOING IN UTAH, AMAZING AYYUB?" Their breathing grew hard together. A sudden jolt shot through Ayyub's body and he looked away from her. "WHY DID THE KOMINAS GO TO THE DESERT? ANSWER ME, AMAZING AYYUB!"

"Keep going."

"I WANT YOU TO TALK TO ME, BABY. YOU HAVE TO TALK . . . TELL ME ABOUT BASIM AND SHAHJEHAN, TELL ME WHAT THE KOMINAS WERE . . ." Ayyub let out a pitiful cry, and she felt his clay lun pump in her hand. With her forehead, she nudged him to look at her, holding eye contact through his orgasm. She pulled her hand out of his pants and noticed a string of spunk hanging between her index and middle fingers. A stupefied Ayyub watched her scoop it up with her tongue.

Then a brown glass bottle sailed past his head. Four psychobilly greaser jinncores, each uniformed in cuffed jeans, a white T-shirt, and a shark-finned quiff, were staring him down. One wielded an upright bass upside down as a potential weapon.

"The Jinn City Rockers!" gasped Ayyub's smokeless-fire girl.

"Forget about the fact that we're going to beat your ass," barked the lead singer. "How do you feel about rebelling against Allah's Qur'an?"

"You're a fucking jinn; what do you care?"

"A lot of jinns are Muslim. We're all Muslim here." His bandmates nodded.

"Well, where in the Qur'an does it say that a jinn can't give hand jobs?"

"For starters, how about An-Nahl, ayat 72? 'And Allah has made wives for you from among yourselves.' 'From among yourselves,' Amazing Ayyub—that means humans."

A crowd formed around Amazing Ayyub and the Jinn City Rockers.

"Marriage between human and jinn is unlawful," said the bass player, turning to the singer. "Who are the authorities?"

"Al-Hasan Al-Basri, Qatadeh, Al-Hakam ibn Uyaynah, Ishaq ibn Rahawei, and 'Uqbeh Al-Assam all agree," the singer replied. "And in Al-Kermani's *Masa'il*, he reports a hadith in which Rasullullah forbade man-jinn marriage."

"I wasn't trying to marry her," Ayyub said under his breath.

"In the *Minyat Al-Mufti 'an Al-Fatawa As-Sirajjiyyah*," said the singer, "Al-Jamal As-Sajstani says, 'Marriage between humankind and jinn is not lawful, for they are of different worlds.' Imam As-Suyuti said that humans and jinns could marry, but there were too many issues to make it advisable.

If a man took a jinn for his wife, would he have to provide her with jinn food, like bones and dung? That's the kind of thing you should think about before you go hooking up at jinncore shows."

"Sajsatani followed the Hanafi madhab," countered a random jinncore from the crowd, "and Suyuti was a Shafi'i. What have you got for the Malikis?"

"In his *Al-Ilhan wa Al-Waswasah*, Abu 'Uthman Sa'id ibn Al-'Abass Ar-Razi related that a group of Yemenis wrote to Imam Malik about a male jinn that had come to them wanting to marry one of their women. The jinn's all, 'I seek to stick to the right path by this proposal.' So Imam Malik tells them, 'I see that there is nothing wrong in doing so, but I dislike to expose this woman to a situation where she might be asked about her husband and she would answer, "It is a male jinn." This may lead to corruption among Muslims.'"

"Imam Malik meant no disrespect towards us," the psychobilly jinn reminded his growing audience, while the Dung Eaters still played onstage. "Both man *and* jinn are Muslims; it says so in the Qur'an."

"Aoudhu billahi mina shaytani rajeem," said Ayyub's jinn girl, loud enough for only Ayyub to hear. "Bismillahir Rahmanir Raheem."

"What are you doing?" Ayyub asked.

"Amazing Ayyub," said the Jinn City Rockers' singer while his band stared the punk down, cracking their knuckles and mashing right fists into left palms, the bassist getting a tight grip on his bass, with dreams of smashing it on Ayyub's brain, "you're an enemy of our community and yours. And you know, the Prophet said that if we see wrong, if we are able, we should first correct it with our own hands . . ." Amazing Ayyub looked desperately to his jinn girl.

"ALLAHU!" she wailed. "LA ILAHA ILLA HU WAL HAYYUL QAYYUM!" The jinns froze in their tracks and put their hands to their ears. "LA TAK'HUDHUHU SINATUN WA LA NAWM," she continued. "LAHU MA FIS-SAMAWATI WA MA FIL'ARD!" Her tajweed, subtly nasal and haunting, drowned out the music, and the jinns howled as though in physical pain. "MAN DHALLADHI YASHFA'U 'INDAHU ILLA BI-IDHNIHI YA'LAMU MA BAYNA AIDIHIM WA MA KHALFAHUM . . ." The power of her recitation spread like a domino effect among the jinncores, plowing through those immediately surrounding her to reach the entire crowd. "WA LA YUHITUNA BI SHAI'IM-MIN 'ILMIHI ILLA BIMA SHA'A WASI'A KURSIYUHUS-SAMAWATI WAL ARD . . ."

Unable to bear the sound, the throngs of jinns became like scattered moths as they turned and fled. Even the Dung Eaters quit their song and ran off just before the stage itself disappeared, and Amazing Ayyub recognized himself as standing in a cemetery once again. "WA LA YA'UDUHU HIFDHUHUMA WA HUWAL'ALIYUL-ADHEEM!" She paused and looked around, observing that the jinns were gone. "Sadaq Allahul'Azeem," she said softly, as an afterthought.

"What the fuck was that?" asked Amazing Ayyub.

"Ayat al-Kursi. A lot of powers in those words, a single ayat equal in weight to a quarter of the whole Qur'an. And it's a surefire way to scare away the jinns—I have sound hadiths on that."

"But if you're a jinn, how could you say it?"

"I'm not a jinn, Amazing Ayyub."

He waited, as though assuming that an explanation would follow, but his smokeless-fire girlfriend said nothing. Her face twitched, then appeared to slowly melt: Her eyes, nose, and mouth slid down her face, turning inward; her streaked pompadour withdrew into her scalp, then reemerged shorter, in a man's cut; and entirely new hair came out of her chin. Her body changed too, her breasts sinking into her heart without a trace. The fishnets became pants, the top a suit coat, shirt, and tie. Eyeglasses grew out of her face to perch on her nose. A white kufi grew out of her brain. Ayyub could only watch with a growing terror in his heart and the taste of vomit in his mouth as the she-jinn morphed into not just any skinny, wormy Caucasian male with a black goatee, but one he could begin to recognize, a rock star–level celebrity evangelist in some small subculture of American life: the Billy Graham of American Muslims.

"HAMZA YUSUF!" screamed Ayyub. "YOU'RE A DUDE! HAMZA YUSUF!"

"Let me explain," said the shaykh in his shrill whine.

"SHAYKH HAMZA YUSUF PRETENDED TO BE A GIRL JINN SO HE COULD BEAT ME OFF!"

"Amazing Ayyub, please . . ."

"YOU FUCKIN' SHAPE-SHIFTING SHAYTAN, I'M NOT A HOMO—"

Hamza Yusuf stopped him with a slap.

"Listen! When I saw you at the jinncore show, I took on that form to get your attention. I've only been out here looking for the great Amazing Ayyub . . . I had to get to you. Astaghfir'Allah, I never intended it to go that far."

"I'm gonna throw up, dude. I'm not a fuckin' homo!"

"You didn't know, Amazing Ayyub. You thought it was a she-jinn who masturbated you. Your niyya was pure."

"Why'd you have to get to me for?"

"I need your help. There's something I have to know."

"What's that?"

"Amazing Ayyub . . . who's killing my zombies?"

"*Your* zombies? What are you talking about, *your* zombies?"

"Of course you understand," said Hamza, stretching a reassuring hand in Ayyub's direction that only made Ayyub flinch, "that there's a great deal of discord in the ummah. We're divided and therefore weak. We fight amongst ourselves, Muslims in conflict with Muslims, all while the United States government is systematically destroying—"

"But after 9/11, you were the one who got all tight with Bush and went cheesedick; you were the one who started using your old, kafr last name and switched your turban for a suit and tie. You're in with them, bro!"

"I did that for the community, Amazing Ayyub."

"So what's with the zombies?"

"Ayyub, we need a more . . . *united* front against Islamophobia. These Progressive-Muslim troublemakers going on Fox News and creating confusion within our mosques are only making it easier for the neocons. Admittedly, zombification of the ummah may not be our most desirable option, but it's the only way to get us through this crucial time . . ."

"And these zombies would all be under you . . . that's some slick shit, Hamza."

"I need to know who's killing them. The zombies should have overtaken our entire community by now. Is it the Kominas, Amazing Ayyub? Have Basim and Shahjehan taken it upon themselves to keep our ummah in shambles?"

"Don't you even say Shahj's name, you bullshit cult leader! Those zombies of yours, they . . . fuck that, I'm not telling you nothin'."

"Have you heard the Kominas' song about Rumi? Where they attack Imam Siraj Wahhaj—one of our most important leaders in North America, our very first brother to perform an Islamic convocation at the House of Representatives?"

"Siraj Wahhaj is a scumbag. I don't like that guy."

"And why's that—because he wants to see Muslims united? Because he shows that Islam is not anti-American? You punk-rocker heretics will ruin everything."

"Whatever, bro. How tits is that, that the last line of defense against your turning Muslims into the walking dead is the fuckin' Kominas?" Amazing Ayyub turned his back on Hamza Yusuf and walked away.

"Can't fool me, Amazing Ayyub," Hamza shouted. "You

thought it was hot, getting jerked off by a jinn . . . like conquering a new territory, wasn't it?"

"Fuck you, Hamza Yusuf, you shape-shifting bone collector! I bet I could have gotten head from you if I'd tried." Ayyub remembered to retrieve his gun before continuing on his way. With the heat in his hands, he almost took out the bad wizard but thought better of it; instead, he sang a new Hamza Yusuf song to the tune of Sham 69's "Hey Little Rich Boy": *Hey, Hamza Yusuf! Take your hand off my cock!* That was all he had for the song, so he just repeated the chorus and laughed until it got old.

The graveyard far behind him, Ayyub reached into his pocket and held his penis, as though enough of his own touch could dilute that of another man. The lun withdrew into him like a frightened turtle—sad penis, poor penis, Ayyub wanting only to console it and rub away the Hamza . . .

Besides shape-shifting to challenge his sexuality on multiple levels, Hamza Yusuf had given Amazing Ayyub room to doubt the taqwacore bands. What if they were just bringing down the ummah? The most legitimate answer might have been that there was no such thing as an ummah, no real collective identity to which everyone with a Muslim name automatically belonged. Maybe if enough Muslims seriously believed in it, there could be an ummah for real, but the taqwacores certainly didn't help at all, pushing away and celebrating division, promoting disunity, offending everyone . . .

Amazing Ayyub wasn't sure if the enemy was within or without, or whether he was right in deciding to murder

Shah 79, who were still at least his Muslim brothers. *But if you're going to really fight your jihad*, he thought, *at least do it with conviction and know that you're right*. Everyone else had a jihad and seemed reasonably confident that it was the right one. Rabeya had driven off the edge of the world with a gun to Matt Damon's head, the Shi'a death-metal band Zulfikar was training to battle Dajjal, whom they believed to be Mullah Omar, the heroes of taqwacore had arrived upon the Utah salt flats to save Islam from zombies, Al Rukn was producing jihadi videos, Shahjehan was giving his life, and Basim was avenging it with a shotgun. Even Hamza Yusuf's creating those zombies might have been a jihad. Then Ayyub wondered how he did it, how Hamza made those horrible, consciousness-destroying taqlidi monsters—maybe with an alien virus from outer space that he had taken off a meteor, or a virus that he'd made himself in his Zaytuna compound. Maybe his playing up Bush had won him access to chemical or biological weapons or a tank of radioactive waste. Or perhaps he'd just said enough zikrs for God to bless him with special powers.

INTERMISSION:

BOMBAY UNGER AND YUSUF ISLAM START A TAQWACORE BAND

I CONCOCTED A purely fictitious Bombay Unger, a fifteen-year-old Persian kid outside a mosque in a Kansas City suburb on a Friday afternoon. He was tying the green laces on his Doc Martens when a community uncle stopped him: "How did you get this name, 'Bombay Unger'? Did you convert to Islam?"

"No, my mom's Muslim. She's from Iran, actually, but my dad's an Irish Catholic."

"And your mother, she married him?"

"Yeah, she married him."

"You know, that is not acceptable in Islam."

"Is that the same with Shi'a? I know this is a Sunni masjid, but we're Shi'a."

"You're Shi'a, brother Bombay?"

"My mom is."

"So she follows the Jafari madhab?"

"I think so."

"You don't know what madhab your mother follows?"

"She didn't tell me."

"Why is your name Bombay?"

"I don't know."

"So what madhab do you follow?"

"Uh, the one you just said, I think."

Then I whisked him to the local record store, where he tried to special-order music by taqwacore bands that he had never actually heard:

"They're called the Mutaweens."

"Okay, I'll look it up. How do you spell that?"

"M-u-t-a-w-e-e-n-s."

"Well, it's not showing. Do you know the label?"

"They're in California, that's all I know."

"Anything else I can help you with?"

"The Bin Qarmats?"

"Spell it?"

"B-i-n, space, Q-a-r-m-a-t-s."

"Don't see it."

"The Zaqqums? Z-a-q-q-u-m-s."

"Nope."

"The Wilden Mukhalloduns? W-i-l-d-e-n, space, M-u-k-h-a—"

"What the hell are these bands?"

"They're taqwacore. You know, the taqwacore scene? In California?"

"Is that anything like Christian rap?"

A dejected and defeated Bombay Unger walked home, arriving just in time to see his mom enter the dining room and deliver his dad a plate with a pig's head on it.

"Thanks, honey." Dad Unger stabbed the pig head with his fork and sawed off a chunk with his knife. "Mom," said Bombay, "I'm gonna start a Muslim punk band."

"You cannot add things to Islam, Bombay. It is already perfect."

"It's not adding anything on—it's only music."

"Why Muslim punk rock? What good does that do? This is what you have to ask yourself, because Allah says, 'I have perfected your religion for you—'"

"I don't know," Dad interjected. "There was Christian metal. You remember Stryper?"

"Bombay," said his mom, "it's bid'ah."

"What's bid'ah?"

"You are following things that are not Islam."

"Mom, Muslim women can't marry non-Muslim men! What about that?"

"Bombay, that was fifteen hundred years ago. Back then, women had no independence, and—"

"Mom, don't you get it? Because you married Dad, I have no right to exist Islamically!"

Bombay Unger was an embarassing little tantrum thrower, a whiny bitch, even, but at fifteen I wasn't any better, stealing those Penguin Korans from the Hobart library to keep dirty kafrs from disrespecting the deen, drawing Khomeini's face on my bedroom wall, and acting all tough about everything. At DeSales High School, I used to bring my Qur'an to biology class and sit there taking my own notes on suras instead of learning about mitochondria. Bombay tuned out his biology teacher to draw flyers in his notebook: "BASS PLAYER WANTED FOR MUSLIM PUNK BAND. MUST BE MUSLIM AND PUNK! CALL BOMBAY UNGER." He wrote his phone number at the bottom and drew an anarchy sign at the top.

The flyer ended up attracting one kid, a clean-cut desi in a Weezer shirt and a Junoon hat, sitting on a picnic table out in front of the school while Bombay, in his Subhumans shirt, tried to preach about the virtues of punk rock for Allah's sake:

"Okay, Yusuf Islam, it looks like you're my man. I hope you're ready, because we're going to turn the whole fucking world on its ear."

"Yeah, man, I'm ready."

"Just straight-up punk rawk, no bullshit."

"Sounds good."

"So, do you actually listen to Muslim punk?"

"What, like that kid from Sum 41? I think he's Hindu."

"Jesus Christ! I'm talking taqwacore."

"What's taqwacore?"

"Like taqwa, core."

"What's 'taqwa' mean?"

"Man, listen (Bombay whipped out the beat-up book, turned to a dog-eared page, and read aloud): I'm at this

Mutaweens show and I'm in the pit, getting tossed around 'n' whatever, and then the music just stops—bam, just like that, it stops—and we stop slamming into each other. Everything just freezes, and all we hear is the singer up there, reciting ar-Rahman as beautiful as I'd ever heard, and he just keeps going with it—the whole sura, you know, all the fabi-ayyi ala irabbikuma tukazibans and shit—and all these hardass punks just stand there listening, and by the time he's done, half of us are in fuckin' tears, bro."

"Wow," gasped Yusuf.

"You got a pair of Doc Martens? You gotta get some Docs and put some green laces in them."

"Why green?" Yusuf asked. Bombay rolled his eyes.

"That's *Muslim* punk. Aren't you Muslim?"

"Of course."

"And this is a punk band. We're Muslim punks; we're taqwacores."

"I have these Vans. Can I wear them with green laces?"

"I suppose you're gonna have to."

So Bombay Unger and Yusuf Islam had a few practices in Yusuf's parents' garage, during which Bombay got the idea to play an adhan on his electric guitar. Yusuf felt as though they should get an imam's approval first, so they headed over to the mosque and the imam sat them down in his office:

"Brothers, the hadith clearly states that musical instruments are forbidden in Islam."

"But how can it get any more Islamic than the call to prayer?"

"Brother Bombay, do you know what happens to the players of instruments?"

Bombay shook his head. The imam opened a large, leather-bound, holy-looking book and flipped to the right page: "'Abu 'Amir or Abu Malik al-Ash'ari narrated that he heard the Prophet, sallallaho alayhe wa salam, say, 'From among my followers there will be some who consider illegal sexual intercourse, the wearing of silk, the drinking of alcoholic drinks, and the use of musical instruments as lawful. And from them there will be some who will stay near the side of a mountain, and in the evening their shepherd will come to them and ask them for something, but they will say to him, "Return to us tomorrow." Allah will destroy them during the night and let the mountain fall on them, and Allah will transform the rest of them into monkeys and pigs, and they will remain so till the Day of Resurrection.'"

"But what about our intentions?" asked Bombay.

"Monkeys and pigs, Bombay. Maybe if you could play your guitar without the strings, that would be better, insha'Allah."

Bombay and Yusuf sat on the steps in front of their masjid, Bombay with his guitar covered in band stickers and the strings taken out. "Don't even worry about it," Yusuf told him. "There are different schools of thought and numerous interpretations."

"It's haram," whined Bombay, looking at his murdered guitar. "This whole thing is like condemning ourselves before Allah."

"Not everyone thinks that music is haram, Bombay."

"We're like monsters." It was almost fun for him to say.

"I mean, the Hanafis believe that it's haram, but maybe the other ones don't."

"We're like fuckin' pariahs."

"I think that Cat Stevens went back to playing guitar, but I'm not sure."

"Yusuf, man, I hope you're ready, they'll be coming after us . . ."

In those notebooks that I had lost in Lowell along with my digital camera, I described Bombay Unger as wearing a Princeton baseball cap turned into a taqwacore qizilbash, with eleven Hot Topic pyramid studs around the sides and one big spike that he stuck through the brim. I even drew a picture of him wearing it, hands in his pockets, slouching like he wanted to be a cool punk so bad . . . but Bombay wouldn't have known enough to even comprehend that he was wearing a qizilbash, that the twelve points represented the Twelve Holy Imams, and the big one in his brim, Imam Husain, Lion of Karbala.

After his failure at the mosque, Bombay's next move was to see his English teacher. He took a boom box into the teacher's empty classroom and played one of his Submumin garage recordings. The song timed in at one minute, nine seconds. The teacher looked at the tiled floor, nodded his head a couple times, and seemed to be considering something quite serious.

"We still don't have a drummer," Bombay said when the music ended.

"Well, Mr. Unger," answered High School English Teacher, "in the wake of 9/11 there's a tremendous opportunity here for a new generation of young Muslims to really bring on a change in perspective regarding Islam's relationship with the West . . . and I'm afraid that you missed that opportunity entirely."

"It was a fuckin' punk-rawk song—what do you want?"

"I want to learn about Islam through your work, Bombay. Defy stereotypes in a productive way, foster understanding, and build bridges. Teach me to see your culture as one of peace and diversity. You know, you could learn something from your classmate Saliha."

"Saliha? What did she do?"

"You know how Muslim girls are supposed to wear that thing on their heads? Well, I've got news for you, Bombay: She doesn't wear it. And she wrote a poem about not wearing that thing that she's supposed to wear, and believe me when I tell you I was completely floored."

"Jesus Christ, man."

"I have such a new outlook on the rich multiculturalism of Islam, and I owe it all to Saliha. She showed me that you can be Muslim and wear blue jeans, and now my eyes have been opened! You see, Bombay, you could be doing that with your music. You can add to the interfaith dialogue that we so desperately need."

"So, yeah," Yusuf Islam told Bombay in the hallway, "I was telling my dad about taqwacore."

"Really? What'd he say?"

"He said the concept was shirk."

"What's shirk?"

"Shirk—you know, because you're taking these bands and following them instead of Allah and His Messenger."

"Oh."

"That's what they call it."

"See, Yusuf? That's why we're punk. We're condemned by everyone."

"I explained it to him, though. I said it wasn't against Islam, it was just music. And I think he got it."

"I'd bet that somebody tries to blow us up at our first show," Bombay snarled.

"He said that whatever talents you have to glorify Allah, you should use them."

"I'd bet somebody tries to cut our heads off."

Bombay went to a kafr party at some kid's house, hoping to forget the imagined condemnations of takfir through visits to a keg and epic ingestion of mushrooms. He was in the kitchen when a jock-looking white boy with a fade haircut and a hooded sweatshirt with Straightedge emblazoned across his chest noticed Bombay and knocked the beer out of his hand.

"What the shit?" yelped Bombay, his voice cracking. "Who the fuck are you?"

"I'm a poison-free independent thinker, that's who. Aren't you supposed to be Muslim?"

"I *am* Muslim," Bombay answered.

"Well, what are you doing with a beer, then? Aren't Muslims edge?"

"I used to be edge."

"Wait, wait . . . no. There's no 'used to be edge.' Either you're edge or you're not edge."

"Then I'm not edge."

"Yeah, you're some fuckin' faggot, pussy, sellout bullshit artist who can't be true to himself and can't even respect his own heritage. That's why we're bombing your shit." Then, like a superhero flying out of the sky, Amazing Ayyub, the Shirtless Shiite Skinhead himself, in the right part of North America at the right time, right there in that kitchen, thrust himself between the two high school boys and blew a spray of beer in the edger's face.

"YOU FUCKER!" The sXe kid lunged at Amazing Ayyub, but surrounding kids held him back. Amazing Ayyub put his arm around a stunned Bombay Unger, and the two walked away, Bombay still unsure of what had just happened and the sXe screaming, "WHY DO YOU THINK MOHAMMAD OUTLAWED BEER, ASSHOLE? YOU SHOULD GO BACK AND READ YOUR FUCKIN' KO-RAN. MAYBE—"

"You're Amazing Ayyub!" Bombay exclaimed out on the back porch, reading the tattoo on his savior's chest. "I know all about you, man—you're a fucking legend! What are you doing out here?"

"I was driving a Shi'a death-metal band on their cross-country tour, and they all died."

"For real? Oh, man, that's crazy!"

"Yeah, I was messed up on speed and Stacker 2. I saw shit

out there in the desert that I don't think was really there, bro. Goin' out of my mind."

"You're nuts, Amazing Ayyub. I'm starting a taqwacore band; I'm tryin' to get it goin', but I'm basically the whole scene out here."

"No shit? What's your band called?"

"The Submumins."

"Submumins? Ha-ha, that's pretty good."

"What's your plan, Amazing Ayyub?"

"Believe in Allah—that's about it."

"You want to be our drummer?"

"Sure, I can drum."

"That's awesome! I can't believe it! Our drummer's fuckin' Amazing Ayyub."

"Who's this girl over here?" Ayyub asked, nodding in the direction of a desi sporting a pink Louis Vuitton purse and a red plastic beer cup and laughing with some white boy.

"That's Saliha," Bombay answered. "She's one of the MSA kids."

"What's she doing here?"

"Same as everyone else."

"SALIHA!" bellowed Amazing Ayyub, who was old enough at that party to be *creepy* old. She turned around. "DID YOU HEAR ABOUT OUR TAQWACORE BAND WE'RE STARTING?" he asked, so loud he overwhelmed everyone around him. "WE'RE THE SUBMUMINS. I'M THE DRUMMER."

"Oh . . . cool."

"WERE YOU TALKING ABOUT ISLAM WITH THAT DUDE OVER THERE? YOU GIVIN' HIM DAW'AH?"

"Whatever," she replied.

"WHERE'S YOUR HIJAB, SISTER?" Ayyub asked with his snort-laugh.

"You don't even know me."

"TELL HIM ABOUT HIJAB, SALIHA. TELL HIM HOW GREAT FUCKIN' HIJAB IS."

"Islam just teaches modesty, you know? Muslim girls don't have to spend all sorts of money on makeup—"

"SO, WHAT? ALLAH JUST GIVES YOU PURPLE EYELIDS FOR ALL THE QUR'AN YOU MEMORIZE?"

"GO TO HELL!" Saliha blurted, turning her back to Ayyub to end the exchange.

"You think she's been done?" Ayyub asked Bombay.

"Saliha? It's hard to say."

"She have a boyfriend? Is she allowed to have boyfriends?"

"I don't know, Amazing Ayyub. You're probably, like, ten years older than her."

"You think she's dirty?"

"I don't think her mind even works that way."

"Man, even sweet Muslim sisters dream of getting bent over."

"You think so?" asked Bombay.

"She'll be a receptacle of the unholy in college, if she's not already. Shit, I bet we missed it by a month."

"She doesn't seem like that type of girl, but who—"

"I'd still give 'er the Zulfikar treatment," Ayyub declared. "You know what I mean? You Shi'a?"

"Yeah."

"Really? That's A-plus, bro. You know about Zulfikar?" Bombay shook his head. "Zulfikar was Imam Ali's sword," Ayyub told him. "One swing, and it'd split you right in half..."

From that night on, Amazing Ayyub lived in Bombay Unger's garage, where Yusuf Islam came by for band practice. One time, Yusuf showed up with a garbage bag full of clothes and presented it to Ayyub.

"They're my dad's," he explained. "He's a professor. He's kind of big; I don't know if they'll fit you."

"Better too big than too small," answered Ayyub, burrowing into the bag to see what he liked. "Don't you worry about a thing, brother Yusuf."

When Bombay Unger finally felt ready to do a show, Amazing Ayyub made a series of long-distance phone calls on Yusuf Islam's parents' phone and brought a handful of taqwacore bands to Kansas City. For a weekend they lived in the garage with Ayyub, drinking bhang lassi and making clumsy Fajr prayers. One band, the Churails, was all girls, with a bass player sporting a classic taqwacore burqa covered in band patches. The whole scene felt too familiar for Amazing Ayyub, but Bombay's wide eyes couldn't stay in his head, and he insisted on living in the garage with the rest of them, pestering the bands for crazy Muslim road stories.

The show went down at the Kansas City Rollerdome, with an audience of maybe two dozen that could be broken down into three components: the local Muslim Student Association clique, a spattering of non-Muslim punks, and the taqwacore bands, watching their comrades. Before their opening set, Bombay Unger presented Amazing Ayyub with a silk-screened Submumins T-shirt. Ayyub pulled it on and swaggered around for a minute, showing how tits it was.

The Submumins took their places with no confidence. Bombay Unger whipped out a green cloth and tacked it on the wall behind them: the Saudi Arabian flag, with an anarchy sign spray-painted on the shahadah.

"That's a nice touch," said Yusuf Islam.

"I had it in my room, but my mom got pissed."

"'Cuz you spray-painted on the shahadah?"

"No, she just hates the Saudis."

"Everyone hates the Saudis," said Yusuf. "I got a Turkish friend, his family's all, 'Fuck the Saudis.'"

"That's a song!" Bombay exclaimed.

"What is?"

"'Fuck the Saudis'—that's totally a song. I gotta write that down." Bombay then turned to the audience. "What's up," he said. "I'm Bombay Unger, this is Yusuf Islam, and that's the one and only Amazing motherfuckin' Ayyub."

"UP THE TAQX!" Ayyub screamed. Members of the other bands roared their approval, but nobody else cared.

"We're the Submumins," Bombay continued. "Maybe you'll like us and maybe you won't, but we could give a fuck either way, because we're not here to be famous rock stars or any of that fake shit—we're punk rock for the deen of Islam!" Then they went into their one-minute songs, Ayyub on the drums, restoring his might as *Amazing* Ayyub, a weathered journeyman of the taqwacores with twenty-five thousand years' worth of scene cred, skin pulled taut over his wiry muscles and old bones.

The Submumins' lead singer recited the only sura he knew—"that one that starts with al-hamdulilahi rabbil'alameen"—trying to make a Minor Threat song out of the Qur'an. Amazing Ayyub watched from behind the drums and wondered if Bombay Unger, whose taqwacore dream had given birth to the whole show and those other bands coming out, would end up leaping off the stage to some dramatic shaheed death in the pit, but there wasn't really a pit at all; the punks just stood there watching him with their hands in their pockets. As the Submumins completed their last song, Unger told everyone off: "ALL YOU FUNDAMENTALISTS OUT THERE, LOOK HERE: IF YOU DON'T LIKE OUR MUSLIM PUNK ROCK, IF YOU WANT TO KILL US LIKE YOU KILLED SALMAN RUSHDIE, THEN WE DON'T FUCKIN' CARE, BECAUSE WE'RE DOING WHAT WE LOVE, SO FUCK YOU!" Someone shouted back that Salman Rushdie was still alive.

Next came the Churails, fronted by a petite desi in a wife beater, wrapped in a giant Palestinian flag, and wearing spiked bracelets. The bass player still had on her riot-grrrl niqab.

Amazing Ayyub and Yusuf Islam blended into the crowd while Bombay Unger stood on the edge, arms crossed.

"As-salamu alaikum," the Churail singer told the audience, getting her salams in return. "This first song is dedicated to Amina Wadud." Once the music started and she let out her improbably deep hardcore voice, the assorted K.C. punks and members of the other taqwa bands started shoving into each other, Ayyub pushing around punks and hardcores who could have been his biological children. After the song they cheered, to which the Churail girl replied with a simple mash'Allah. She told everyone that her next song was about something that had happened last week in Gaza. At some point during the song, someone's boot caught Amazing Ayyub in the head. Ayyub flipped out, throwing fists everywhere, until the kids held him back and got him out of the pit so he could calm down. Then he spotted Bombay standing off to the side near the MSA faction.

"Kids today," said Ayyub.

"Dammit," said Bombay Unger. "Dammit, Amazing Ayyub, dammit, I wish I was a poor little Muslim girl. The media's gonna be all over her: So you sing in a punk band, but you're a Muslim girl? How do you reconcile wearing spiked bracelets with being a Muslim girl? What response have you received from Muslims for being a girl in a band, and for not having that thing on your head, and how can you be a Muslim girl singing at punk shows in the wake of 9/11, and as a Muslim girl punk rocker trying to live Islam out loud, how do you feel about the war in Iraq? Fuck, man. If I was a poor little Muslim girl, I'd be a millionaire by now."

"Forget about it, brother—that bitch is a tuna helper. I can tell just by looking at her."

"Man . . . I'm trying to start something real here, I'm trying to be creative, and all she does is—"

"You throw that girl a cock, she'll throw it right back! I'd bet you any kind of money. But you throw her a puss, she'll lap it up."

"You think so, Amazing Ayyub?"

"I'd straighten her out; don't you worry about a thing. I'd pull her soul out through her snatch. Remember Zulfikar, bro, ha-ha . . . oh, shit, that's the name of our next song: 'Remember Zulfikar'—that sounds cool, right?"

After the failed show, the Submumins couldn't stand to be around each other, so Bombay Unger went home to sit on his parents' roof and inhale a can of WD-40, Yusuf Islam went home to chat online with Naseeb.com girls, and Amazing Ayyub, because he had no home anywhere, just walked around town in that homemade Submumins T-shirt, still carrying his big gun and his garbage bag of secondhand professor's clothes. He considered shooting at squirrels he saw but decided against it, since a gun like that could do damage to someone's house. Spotting a squirrel on a stone ledge, Ayyub gently put his gun down, picked up a fallen branch, eased his way over, and swung the branch down fast. The squirrel got away, and Ayyub's weapon only whacked the stone.

"Cocksucker!" he growled. "Next time I'll kill your whole family."

Then he saw the MSA gang standing around, talking by one of their cars.

"You see," droned the MSA's Fonz apparent, "it's haram for a muqallid to do ijtihad, the same way that it's haram for a mujtahid to do taqleed." The other kids nodded like zombies. Amazing Ayyub went over to them and just stood there, waiting for someone to acknowledge him. Saliha rolled her eyes at the oversize machine gun resting on his shoulder.

"Salam alaikum," said Amazing Ayyub.

"Wa alaikum as-salam," replied the MSA kids.

"I'm going on a hajj to Buffalo," Ayyub announced. They laughed at him.

"Buffalo counts for hajj?" one scoffed.

"I think Khaled Abou El Fadl said it's okay," smirked another.

Then came Saliha's turn to wisecrack: "Yeah, like Khaled Abou El Fadl is an authority? Nigga please!"

On his last day in Kansas City, Amazing Ayyub sat on the ground with Bombay Unger, the Churails' bassist, and Harun, the zine-writing nomad, in front of Your Service Station, a gas station owned by the *United* Nation of Islam (UNOI), the local heresy. It looked like a regular spot to pump gas at, but instead of the big Mobil or Hess logo looming atop a tall signpost were a white star and crescent on a red field, with the current gas prices underneath. The UNOI had been started by an African American truck driver and janitor named Royall Jenkins whom angels had abducted and flown across the universe in their spaceship one day in the 1970s. The MSA kids didn't go to his gas station.

"When I start a new band," said Bombay Unger, "I'm going to call it the Amazing Ayyubs."

"Fuck that," said Ayyub. *La fata illa Ali*, he thought.

"So you're going to Buffalo," said the Churails' bass player, glancing at Ayyub's big gun lying across the curb.

"I gotta straighten that shit out, balance the fuckin' see-saw. But I might go to Chicago first."

"Michael Muhammad Knight lives in Buffalo," the bass player remarked. "Do you know him?"

"Fuckin' A, I lived on his couch!"

"Well, if you see him, ask him why he can't develop any of his female characters."

"All right," said Ayyub.

"Plus, he's got a serious identity fetish."

They had nothing to do but sit and waste blood like clustered gutter punks, but the famous Junayd had spoken of Sufism as just sitting for an hour with Allah and having no worries. Harun and Ayyub related past adventures, quotes from a funny taqwacore movie that nobody had ever seen, and stories about bands that didn't even exist anymore and, for all anyone knew, may have never existed at all—bands with no recordings, no T-shirts, no surviving show flyers, no ticket stubs bearing their name, and no one in that particular parking lot to corroborate the accounts.

Harun wanted to take pictures for his zine's Kansas City scene report, so Bombay and the Churail girl stood up and Ayyub stayed on the ground. Bombay leaned up against Your Service Station with his back and one foot on the window, put up a middle finger, and aimed it behind him, maybe at the UNOI. The Churail picked up Ayyub's gun to pose with. It was bigger than she was but seemed light enough in her hands. She reminded Ayyub of the original niqabi riot grrrl, Rabeya, pointing her normal-size AK-47 at Matt Damon. This Churail girl stared off to the side, as though surveying a situation just outside of Harun's shot, while Bombay lowered his gaze to the concrete and only Amazing Ayyub looked directly at the camera—no snarl or pout or anything, no posture, just simple Ayyub Masoom of the Muhibbin, the Sabirin, the Zahidin, the Mu'minin, the Muqinin, the Qani'in, the Sa'ihin, the Radiyin, the 'Arifin, and the Salihin, with his clear plastic garbage bag of professor clothes . . .

After the picture, Amazing Ayyub got up to take his leave of Harun, the Kansas City taqwacore scene, and the United Nation of Islam gas station, with its giant red-and-white crescent signs, and headed for the bus station, an insanely long way away. Once, I too was at the K.C. Greyhound and was hoping to walk to the UNOI, but someone told me that it'd be too far a journey that would cross various terrible neighborhoods. I ended up tapping out, but not Ayyub—he just mosied along with his gun on one shoulder and the bag of clothes on the other, never complaining about the walk, nobody fucking with him. He kept himself and his qareen company by singing songs: first his favorite, Sham 69's "Hey Little Rich Boy," and then California taqwacore songs, like the "Ballad of Walid Al-Taha," an abrasive but sentimental pure punk hymn that Osama Van Halen could bust out in under a minute. Amazing Ayyub knew all about Walid Al-Taha and the Moorish Orthodox Church from driving Osama Van Halen around on their tour. Ayyub had grown tight enough with the band that at one show they'd put him onstage and done "Last Resort," putting Ayyub's name in the lyrics while he stomped around: *Oi, oi, Ayyub, get your hair cut!*

The MOC made for a great concept, the singer had told him, but the execution came off as too hippie for his own taste. What it really needed was all those angry, anarchist street-punk Islamophile kids who loved Hakim Bey.

Amazing Ayyub had no money for a bus ticket, but once he got to the station he could read his sura, go invisible, and smuggle himself and his big gun on. If the bus were packed, he could hide himself in the restroom or the aisle, or maybe even climb on seats to get up into the overhead luggage area. It's not anything punk, but I feel for Ayyub like I feel for Axl Rose in the video for "Estranged." The video shows Axl on a big oil tanker in the middle of the ocean, wearing that Charles Manson T-shirt that he used to wear, and I just have this feeling that Axl has gone through a lot to reach that point in the story, even though there really is no story. Anyway, Axl climbs up on the railing, pauses for a moment to reflect on whatever's happened to bring him there—knowing all of the chaos and knowing that after just this little more, it will slow down forever—and then jumps overboard. His band tries to save him; I can't remember who throws him the life preserver (maybe Izzy), but Axl catches it and throws it back. The drummer or someone rows out in a lifeboat, but the waves are crashing all around him and he can't get near Axl. So Axl is all alone and drowning in the ocean until Allah sends some dolphins to save him. At the end of the video, he just sits there, wrapped up in a towel, with a dolphin next to him, and smirks, like, *Fuck you. I'm Axl Rose and I can kill myself and live through it.*

So Amazing Ayyub, walking to the Kansas City Greyhound station, knowing that soon enough he'd be in Buffalo, felt like Axl Rose might have felt—not Axl after he gets saved by the dolphins, but Axl when he jumps.

TAQWACORES vs.

THE ISLAMIC SOCIETY OF NORTH AMERICA

IN THE LATE summer came ISNA's annual convention, and I imagined Amazing Ayyub riding a
Greyhound there to lurk among the bazaar crowds
under his invisibility purdah, maybe sit in on a few lectures,
and still carry that massive invisible gun of his, the banana
clip long and curvy like an old Arab scimitar from *Thousand
and One Nights* fantasies.

ISNA's events are always swarming with Islam-oriented
hip-hop, which may present an interesting quirk to non-
Muslims but offers no frightening honesty, no open challenge, and certainly no heresy. One year some desi kid
sold me a CD based on his boast that his rap crew had the
"number-one daw'ah song in the country." Does Billboard
have daw'ah charts now? It was off the hook, he told me.

Every one of his songs began with a Malcolm X sample. The next year I found a white, non-Muslim Islamophile walking around ISNA with a press pass, announcing that Islam was in a state of massive cultural upheaval because Muslim kids in Malaysia listened to heavy metal.

The taqwacore bands had thrown together a comp CD and called it *Hamza Don't Surf*. Basim pressed a mess of copies, and I brought a pile of *The Taqwacores*, wrapped protectively in my Wesley Willis hoodie. After walking four miles to the gas station, I met up with the Kominas, Aziz Aziz, and Shahjehan's dad, who had rented a van. I climbed in and we took I-90 to Chicago, driving through the night and arriving shortly after 6:00 AM.

Shahjehan's dad and Aziz retired to their respective hotels while I went with the Kominas to the Donald E. Stephens Convention Center. The place was set up and ready but completely deserted, so we ran wild in the empty bazaar, jumping on tables and singing taqwa songs loud. I had a pile of counterfeit badges with names like Ben Ishmael and Al Rukn but wasn't sure if they'd do the job later, so Shahjehan went behind the media booth and added our names to a Post-it list of registered journalists. Then we went upstairs, napped for a few hours on the couches, and went back down as things were livening up. We approached the media booth and told them that we needed badges. The guy running things looked at his little yellow Post-it, saw our names, and wrote them up. Now we had all-access media passes.

Omar tipped us off about the press conference featuring

Karen Hughes, Department of State undersecretary of public diplomacy and George W. Bush's representative to the ISNA convention, and ostensibly centering on an earth-shattering announcement about a brochure condemning terrorism. Hughes elevated the affair to engage ISNA stars Nur Abdullah, Ingrid Mattson, and Sayyid Syeed in a mutually meaningless hand-job session: Islam is great, America is great, American Muslims contribute to American life in so many ways, American Muslims love America, America loves its American Muslims, rich fabric of diversity, beautiful mosaic of cultures, forging partnerships for the future, and so on and bullshit forever.

It was obvious, not least of all to those charged with protecting the event, that we didn't belong in there. A police officer and big man in a suit came over and asked us to step outside. Just beyond the door, the big man flashed his badge and said, "Special Agent, U.S. State Department." He had us open our bags, then compared our ISNA passes with our driver's licenses, making me glad I hadn't used my Bombay Unger badge.

"Who do you write for?"

"*Muslim WakeUp*," I told him.

"What's that?"

"It's an online magazine. I've written for it for three years now, and these guys are with me." The agent turned to an ISNA official, who vouched for us. We got our IDs back and made a mildly awkward return to the press conference. As it wrapped up and everyone filed out, the ISNA guy smiled and apologized for harassing us. "You just need proper attire," he said. Then he went over and told Shahjehan that he was okay, but that they didn't understand my Alternative Tentacles work jacket. Instead of just asking me what it meant, they went ahead and sent a special agent after us, but what can you do? Next came a whole other press conference devoted to the issue of ISNA's *Horizons* mag on African American Islam, but nearly all the reporters and photographers had followed Hughes out. Too bad they missed poet Amir Sulaiman as he got up and delivered his famous "Dead Man Walking," which no less than buried all the slick, generic pomp of the previous affair as he told us how he couldn't speak of "shahadahs, Qur'ans, and homemade bombs, but the president can drop A-bombs and napalm." First time I heard those lines was at a vegan punk show in Oakland.

Perhaps the most traditionally religious of us, Shahjehan left for Zuhr prayer—if it hadn't been a Friday, I would have joined him, but I just wasn't in the right frame of mind for an ISNA khutbah. Basim and I sat in the food court, and Shahjehan came back after making his sunna rakats, saying that it didn't feel right, so we hit the bazaar.

HijabMan was there again, selling T-shirts to fund his overseas imam study. This year he'd stepped up his game to include twisting long balloons into animal shapes. Basim said that he'd better not make a balloon dog, or balloon angels wouldn't enter the convention center. HijabMan made himself a pretty massive balloon hat, and it was just fun to watch him work his magic with whoever walked by.

For some time, the Kominas and I claimed an empty space next to his booth, tossing all of our books and CDs on the floor and writing the prices on a piece of Styrofoam. I imagined Amazing Ayyub wandering through the bazaar, maybe under the cloak of his invisibility spell, stumbling across the booth for Yazid TV, the new all-Muslim channel, and overhearing mention of Shah 79's upcoming performance at the Yazid studios in Amherst, New York, a suburb of Buffalo.

Shahjehan later went to his dad's hotel while Basim and I hung out with a hijabi anarchist girl, wearing a Rage Against the Machine T-shirt (I won't say her real name; I'll call her Ayesha, after the Malice song), and her friend. They both wore volunteer badges that they hadn't stolen. After a while, their boss came over and said that ISNA head Ingrid Mattson had seen them slacking, so they'd better go circulate. We tagged along, and the four of us wound up discovering a way to the outside balcony. Shahjehan saw us from the sidewalk and ran up, along with Aziz and one of his friends, and the seven of us had a balcony party with juice and cookies (purloined from the speakers' lounge) before everyone had to go do their thing. At the end it was just the Kominas, kings of ISNA, and me, leaning over the railing and watching girls below. They couldn't hear us, but we sang 8-bit songs: "This ain't a put-on or a verse out of the Qur'an . . ."

Friday night, Ayesha joined us on the top floor of the parking garage, and we watched the ISNA crowd from something like five stories up. In a hotel window across the street, we saw some girls bhangra dancing. They stopped when we waved at them.

The Kominas and I slept in the garage that night. Cops woke us up at maybe eight thirty the next morning.

"Are you guys okay?" one asked. "We had a report of a man down."

"We were just taking a nap," I told him.

"You guys have hotel rooms?"

"Of course." He walked away, and it took me a second to register what a dumb exchange we had just shared.

The Muslim Students Association was holding its parallel conference in the Hyatt across the street. On Saturday night the group hosted a lecture called "Death: The Journey of a Lifetime" with Mokhtar Maghroui. "The Prophet (sal-lallaho alayhe wa salam) advised us to remember death often," read the program, "to visit graves and reflect on what we cannot see but must inevitably experience." I rode to Burr Oak Cemetery with the Kominas and Muhammed Al-Ahari El. Muhammed's a well-known and well-traveled cat in American Muslim stories. He mastered the traditions of the Moorish Science Temple and the Moorish Orthodox Church, attended FOI meetings in Harlem and the Blackstone Rangers' mosque in Chicago, and in the 1980s even had an encounter with Azreal, the Five Percenters' death angel.

We were looking for the resting place of noble Drew Ali—the son of runaway slaves, adopted son of Cherokees, initiate of the Egyptian mysteries, prophet on a giant button that Basim stuck on his baseball cap. But after spending two hours roaming the cemetery in search of Ali's grave without flashlights, we followed Muhammed in a special Moorish prayer and then squeezed back out through the gate. Back at the convention, the hungry Kominas and I entered the food court, walking by each table and scavenging food from abandoned Styrofoam containers. Girls who looked like they'd been the popular kids back in seventh grade treated us with the kind of disdain befitting their type, but then a brother called us over and offered us some of his meal.

Later, Ayesha threw cushions at me on the second floor of the Doubletree Hotel while I tried to defend some unacceptable opinions. Basim came through, and we wrestled on the couches. We met up with Shahjehan and Ayesha's friend, who had a bag of equality, so we all walked back to her car and elevated. With Hassan bin Sabbah and such, there was enough shared history between cannabis and Sufis to make for a decent conversation if I had remembered any of it, but I could at least say that I owned a legitimate silsila, lineage, having been taught how to smoke by Azreal, who himself was taught by the Five Percenters' Allah, the former Clarence 13X. I could read on Shahjehan's face that getting high with muhajabahs at the ISNA convention had reconciled two opposing worlds for him, that it was all okay and made sense now. We climbed out of the car, and I tossed myself lazily into the nearby mesh fence as if I were in a steel-cage match.

The weeded taqwacores stumbled back to the Hyatt and wandered through the Club ISNA scene: girls in sparkling hijabs and ass pants; guys Basim called "desi guidos" sporting hair gel and button-ups. I felt as if we had fallen into a Naseeb ad. Intermixed with the ten million smiling young professionals floated a smattering of Muslim hipster T-shirts: My Name Causes International Security Alerts; Muslims Do It Five Times a Day; Brown Trash; I am FOB. Then there was one with a picture of a boat and the caption This Is How We Got Here. I looked at Basim and told him that I did in fact have a thought about all of this, but my brain had slowed down and I couldn't do anything with it. Then I saw a guy's homemade shirt that broke down the acronym ISNA as I'm Single 'n' Available and offered his phone number on the back.

We meandered with the girls and spent some time sitting down in the elevator, yelling nonsense at people each time it opened on a new floor. We finally picked a floor and got off to sit outside the elevator while random kids entered and exited our cipher. Shahjehan told me that he could sell my book, so I said sure; he took a copy to peddle and accidentally found himself in an argument with some guy over whether there could be different ways of praying. The brother told us all that we needed to learn our Islam, and I wanted to tell him that Elijah Muhammad had said that a new Islam was on its way and would come via pamphlets in English and Arabic, dropped to Earth from the Motherplane, but I wasn't sure how he'd receive it, so I let him go back to his old Islam, whose time was running out. At 3:24 AM, we were still sitting by the elevator when out came Omar from the Muslim boy band 786. By then there were several girls in our crew, and they all begged him to sing, so he asked what song they wanted. Someone asked for "Make Du'a," so he busted out a few lines, and then the Joey Fatone of a thousand ISNA conventions went on his way.

Rumors of a party in one of the rooms never materialized, and the group split up. I went with the Kominas to search for a place to sleep, finally deciding on an MSA lecture room. Under the stage, it was dark and we could stretch out and sleep hard without worrying about anyone seeing us. Shahjehan had on an MSA shirt that he had found, but it was a girls' shirt and said Sisterhood across the front. With my bag for a pillow, I knocked out to Basim singing a taqwacore Ramones tribute, "The MSA Took My Baby Away."

By the time I woke up, Shahjehan had left and a lecture was taking place over my head: "Holding on to the Rope of Allah—Repentence, Forgiveness, and Du'a," again with Mokhtar Maghroui. I could have crawled out from the front of the stage and made an odd scene, but Basim was still asleep so I just stayed there and listened. It was actually pretty good; Mokhtar kept it simple and heartfelt and delivered the talk in almost a tender whisper. Through it all, I looked at the big, safety-pinned Vote Hezbollah patch on my rucksack—a picture of a Muslim man sitting in julus from one of those how-to-pray booklets, with spiked hair added—and as Mokhtar spoke of there being no tauba without tears, no repentance without earnest desire, Taqwa Man we called him. I imagined Taqwa Man in that julus, working his inner discipline. Taqwa Man had good prayer posture, the straight spine of a man who knew what he was doing.

Vote Hezbollah's Kourosh was our blood and guts, but he hadn't been able to make it out to ISNA because of issues he had gotten into with his parents. There was always something—one time, his mom found his mushrooms and then threw away all of his song notebooks and Ayatollah shirts. He records all of his songs alone in his room, sometimes under parental house arrest. Kourosh's contribution to the *Hamza Don't Surf* comp was a rendition of my poem "Muhammad Was a Punk Rocker." In the Vote Hezbollah version, Kourosh replaces my Rancid reference with a shout to the Fearless Iranians from Hell. Basim said that when he reads the poem now, he hears it in Kourosh's voice.

Instead of paying a combined $180 to go to the Naseeb Meet-Up down the street, we hit the CTA and went into the city to visit a Five Percenter I knew named Jura Shaheed Allah. Over beers, the Kominas heard Jura do the knowledge. He said that Chicago had a special kind of energy, which we all readily recognized.

The Nation of Gods and Earths is open, said Jura, and anyone can be a Five Percenter. There are some who read the Qur'an, but others might study the Bible or Tao Te Ching. One is not more "five percent" than the other. We exchanged our peace, and he wished us a safe journey. Then it was back to the CTAs that Wesley Willis sang about.

At the Hyatt I threw down my bag and took a seat in the corner while Basim and Shahjehan made their tawafs around the scene. At one point, a Shi'a girl I had met at the previous year's convention came over, and we talked about Amina Wadud's woman-led prayer. I told her that deep down, the woman-led-prayer people were still pretty safe in their religion, and their agenda wasn't at all to destroy orthodoxy (and that could be taken as good or bad).

My conversation with the Shi'a turned to Muhammad; she told me that the Prophet was a perfect human being, and I answered that such ideas were why I had abandoned Christianity. Among Buddha's unruly friends were medieval Zen heretics who called him a dry turd on a stick and burned holy scriptures, and they were actually devout Buddhists who only wanted to kick out the crutches. Rather than a "Progressive Muslim" movement, we needed some of that serious lunacy . . . instead of hippie-dippy Goofy Sufis, we needed orders like the dead Malamatiyya ("Blameworthy Ones"), with shaykhs like Mad Mehmet, who'd get high and wave a bottle of wine as he humped Rumi's tomb. *Time* magazine had it wrong: that "battle for the soul of Islam" had already gone down; the sanitizing forces had claimed victory long ago.

Shahjehan got hammered and put himself in the middle of a sheesha party, and a jolly Basim came back to me every now and then to offer his commentary. During one visit, he sat down and wrote on my napkin in big letters, "I'll see you after the club."

"This is what we'll tell the girls," he said.

"What girls?"

"All the girls we happen to talk to in the next eight hours." Then Shahjehan came through and told me of some guy walking around with a sign that read: Remember, Allah Is Watching. It looked like Shahj was getting depressed and didn't know why. On more or less the same page, I took out my phone and started calling sisters who weren't there. Inur had given a talk at the MSA conference but had had to go back home early, and she understood the gloom of watching Club ISNA from the outside. My call woke her up, so I let her go and woke up someone else: a desi ex-girlfriend back home who laughed at my ISNA conventioneering and said she'd never go in a million years. She had just come back from India and had a cream-colored shalwar kameez waiting for me when I got home. Then I called Helena, my ISNA girlfriend for the previous two years, who had skipped this year's convention for a road trip to New York.

Two girls walked by us in matching HijabMan shirts—Good Things Come in Small Pakis—and I told Basim that I've been that good thing once or twice. I was even accused of being one of those white convert guys who fetishize brown girls, and my only defense was that the Arab guys fetishize white convert girls, so it all evens out.

Such a phenomenon undeniably exists among the white boys, and I'm pretty sure that I've gone down that road.

There's a certain kind of blue-eyed kafr who converts and automatically gets hung up on the skinny virgin princesses with diamond Allahs around their necks. Whether he'll admit it or not, the Muslim community becomes a new way to go after the same old bullshit. What he wants is a timid little thing who'll make him gulab jamuns and look at his dick like it's going to kill her, and then in paradise he'll get seventy-two Japanese schoolgirls like Kagome on *InuYasha*.

The Kominas went for the kinds of girls who were available in their respective circles. Back in Massachusetts, Basim was a local goth-punk hero, so he got with the goth white girls. With his mohawk and leather jacket covered in patches and paint, he was too much a deliberate failure for the desis. At the other end, Shahjehan was the kid who brought us to Bilal Musharraf's house for dinner. He could put on a Lord & Taylor exterior, do coke with girls from the mosque, and sneak into the secret lives of doctors' daughters.

We eventually pulled ourselves up, met up with Ayesha and her friend, and left the Hyatt together. We all piled into the friend's car, put on our *Hamza Don't Surf* CD, and peeled out while blaring "Rumi Was a Homo" with the windows down. The girls took us into the city and up Devon's Little India strip of stores and restaurants, still playing the taqwacore songs, Shahjehan singing along at the top of his lungs. Crumpled in the backseat, feeling like a ninety-year-old man with my bad posture, I squinted against the wind and watched the muhajabahs in front dancing to "Ayesha": *Oh, Ayesha, surf's up . . .*

Ayesha hangs ten, but not Hamza—not no more.

I turned to Basim and said in his ear, "Isn't this some shit?" and that was about as well as I could articulate my observation. Something strange was happening—a crazy taqwa-punk dream turning real, a whole new scene of cast-offs—but it was legit, as far as we could tell. We ended up on the rocks by Lake Michigan, falling in and out of sleep. At half-awake times, I looked at the kids around me and fully loved Chicago, where Noble Drew Ali had moved his temple because he said it was closer to Islam and we'd find the new Mecca there. I revisited my old dream of Basim, with his mohawk sculpted to make Arabic letters and spell Allah's name down the middle of his scalp, then imagined Shahjehan playing an electric-guitar adhan like Jehangir Tabari on these rocks—and he could really do it. I had heard him play the call back in Boxborough with a guitar that once belonged to Salman from Junoon. Isn't that some shit, too.

F. SCOTT FITZGERALD

VS.

FIVE DESI GIRLS

 IT'S BAD NEWS when you're lying in bed with one arm pinned under a sleeping Muslimah and want only to punch yourself in the face with your free hand, so you just lie there through the night and think about it. So much tension builds inside you that you're afraid your nervous energy alone will wake her up, even though you haven't moved.

There were times when all I wanted was to be something for a Muslimah besides her terrible secret, but that wouldn't be happening here. Unfit as a prop for her to whip out at family Eid dinners back home, I was good only for her Binghamton dorm bed, hundreds of miles from anyone who could know. It made no sense to fall for a girl with community issues until I found something to offer the community, but those odds were long and she knew it. Her kisses would often become aggressive, almost an attack, as though the kisses themselves could be a violent act upon her aunties. Then, without warning, she'd stop and pull away, sometimes in tears. Back and forth we'd go through the night, until we both gave up. The community wins again . . .

I remembered the unpainted doghouse at Herman Street that I had filled with LJN wrestling dolls, imagined burning it with all of them inside as a takiyeh, swirling black smoke rising from the melting rubber Hulk Hogans and Macho Mans. I thought of Moulana Zakariyah saying that Hazrat Shah Ishaq Muhajiree Makki told Imdadullah Mujahir Makki to "regard yourself to be most inferior in the entire creation." The old dog who'd once lived in that doghouse must have felt reasonably shitty about life; Herman Street might have gotten the poor thing so down on itself that it became a Sufi saint. I didn't feel so great either.

The girl had already expressed concern over my stories and how they'd look to her family someday, declaring, "No more 'Oh, look at me, I'm too cool for ISNA'; no more negative attention."

"What do you mean, 'negative attention'?"

"It's not only for my sake. You wrote this great book about the Five Percenters, you put all that time into the research and tracking down the people and interviewing them, and you want it to be taken seriously, right?"

"Sure."

"And get it out through a nice university press or something, right? But no one will take you seriously if you keep writing the crazy stuff." With her asleep on my better arm, I thought about wrestlers like Sabu, who'd get tangled up in barbed wire and refuse to ask the referee for help because that meant breaking character, Cactus Jack getting his face stomped into thumbtacks by Terry Gordy, Terry Funk getting burned by the Sheik, Atsushi Onita fighting Mr. Pogo with land mines scattered around the ring. I remembered the classic garbage wrestlers, their foreheads mangled with deep razor-cut grooves, matam of a kind . . . and I wondered what the literary equivalent of that could be—how a writer might get to injure himself for his craft. Perhaps by writing so hard that it makes him a loser in every other part of his life: dropping out of college, losing jobs, losing girlfriends, living on Herman Street as a twenty-five-year-old, squatting illegally in a Buffalo State residence hall at twenty-six, sleeping in his car at twenty-seven, crawling back to Mom's house in self-defeat, bumming on professors' couches, and never going anywhere, never wanting anything else but to look at a shelf full of books with his name on the spines and say, "I'd rather have this than a nice house; I'd rather have this than a nice girl, no matter how much it hurts to be alone."

Or perhaps by writing himself into his stories as a complete asshole of a character. The Eleventh Imam, Imam Hasan al-Asgari, said, "It is so ugly for a believer to follow a passion that causes him humiliation," but al-Hallaj said that after attaining self-effacement, people reach a station where effacement and affirmation cease to exist. The master of the iron clawhold, Fritz Von Erich, told his sons to pay the price that the other man wasn't willing to pay. Baudelaire wrote that "the more a man gives to his art, the less he fornicates," but I think that's the least of it. Approach your work as if you were Cactus Jack, and then one of your stories becomes the Undertaker, the one who throws you off the roof of the cage through a table, and one's Shoji Nakamaki, who shoves you onto a bed of nails; one's Big Van Vader—fighting him gets your head caught up in the ropes and your ear ripped off—and one's Terry Gordy, power-bombing you onto thumbtacks. One's Eddie Gilbert, who breaks a wine-cooler bottle on your skull, and one's Terry Funk, whom you fight in an exploding-time-bomb, barbed-wire King of Death match; and, of course, one's the Rock, who cuffs your hands behind your back, then brains you seventeen times with a folding chair. And look at you now: scars all over your body, short-term-memory loss from your concussions, a missing ear, floating bone chips in your arm. Then, when you've already completely destroyed yourself, along comes Carlito, chewing on his apple, and he spits it all in your face.

On her headboard she had a copy of *Lipstick Jihad*, written by an Iranian American journalist about going back to Iran after so many years. Can't remember the author's name, but the front cover had a picture of a woman in a hijab, wearing sunglasses and holding a cell phone to her ear. That'd make a compelling dichotomy for some casual browser of Barnes & Noble, I imagined: *She wears that thing on her head, but she has a cell phone . . . it's like East and West, Islam and the Modern World!*

When it came to my community girl, the other shoe finally dropped around the same time that a British publishing house bought the U.K. rights to my Muslim punk-rock novel. It was starting to get cold in upstate New York, I had no more reason to stick around the Binghamton campus, and now I had $750, so I bought a two-week Greyhound pass, intending to head south. The first stop, however, was Syracuse, where I had an Indian ex-girlfriend, Fatima, who after the semester ended wouldn't be around anymore. I needed to see her while I could. When we'd first gotten together, she'd been eighteen and a freshman, just coming off her hijab phase, and disgusted with the Hamza Yusufs of her scene. Back then she'd been terrified of being a girl-friend, unsure of what it meant, not quite decided on what she could or couldn't do with a boy. After we broke up, she got drunk once and smoked weed maybe twice. She did a semester in India, met a guy there, lost her virginity, and came back.

I stood in front of her house and called her phone. She came out and we hugged. She took me inside to meet her roommates, one white and one desi.

"Are you hungry?" asked the white one.

"Yeah, I'm kind of hungry," I answered.

"Does he want to eat?" she asked Fatima.

"We're actually on our way to get food," Fatima replied.

The roommate laughed about the misunderstanding, and Fatima led me toward the door, stopping when she remembered something. I stood around while she ran up the stairs and came back down with my cream-colored shalwar kameez. "I almost forgot," she said.

"This is great. Thank you!"

"I hope it fits. You can wear it at next year's ISNA convention."

"I'd totally wear it, but I'm not sure if there's another ISNA for me."

"Why not?" she asked, opening the door.

"I'm getting old," I answered as we stepped out. "I can't be that old, sketchy guy in the hotel lobby, trying to mack on ISNA girls." A little ways down the sidewalk, I thought of a question: "How's the boy?"

"He's good."

"Are you going to miss Syracuse?"

"Sure. It still hasn't hit me yet."

"What's your plan?"

"I'm going home for two weeks, and then I'm going to Delhi."

"Delhi?" This was the first time in the dialogue that I'd looked straight at her. "You're going to fucking Delhi?"

"I didn't tell you about that?"

"You told me you were thinking about it."

"I got the job, and I'm going."

"What's the job again?"

"It's an NGO."

"What's that?"

"Like a not-for-profit . . ." Her explanation trailed off.

"Holy shit," I said. "Delhi."

"Delhi," she said.

"And that's where he is."

"Yeah, our parents actually want us to get engaged."

"Are you serious?"

"It's just a way for us to live in the same city without me being thought of as a slut."

"So, it's a social formality—you're not really engaged."

"Well . . ."

"Fatima, you're twenty-two!"

"That makes me an old maid in some places."

"Could you see yourself marrying this boy?"

"Yes," she replied without hesitation.

"Okay."

She walked me to a pita place on a small strip of restaurants and stores. The crowd inside and the neighboring businesses told me that we weren't far from the campus. The place was so packed with SU kids that we took our pitas outside and sat on the sidewalk.

"I owe you for this," she said.

"You paid."

"No, I mean for us sitting on the sidewalk. I never did that before meeting you." It sounded to me like a eulogy on our friendship.

"Yeah," I said.

"So, how are the girls treating you?" she asked.

"Eh, I don't know. Did I tell you about the girl at Binghamton?"

"You started to, I think. Was she desi?"

"Yeah, she was desi."

"What happened?"

"She has these parents, you know, and a community, and I'm whatever it is I am. I don't know what else to say about it."

"Those desi girls," she smirked. "They're nothin' but trouble."

"I'm trouble for them, too, I guess."

"Do you even date non-Muslims anymore?"

"I barely have non-Muslim friends," I told her. "Is that weird? I pull this heretical shit, but in the end I'm as entrenched as anyone."

"Well, I wouldn't go that far. You don't have family expectations to worry about."

"My family might love to see me drunk at Christmas — it'd be the most normal thing I've done." She laughed. For a clumsy moment, neither of us had anything left to say, so we stared away in opposite directions.

"So, what are you writing these days?" she asked.

"I'm writing myself as a fictional character."

"It's about time," she said.

"What does that mean?"

"You made fiction of me a long time ago."

"Oh, shit, Fatima. I guess I did."

"Yeah, and you know what?"

"What?"

"My dad is on these South Asian literature listservs, and he forwards me posts about books he thinks I'd like, and they were talking about your novel! So he emailed me and was all, 'Fatima, have you ever read this? Do you know about these Muslim punk rockers? It might be interesting.' If he only knew."

"Good thing he doesn't."

"Yeah."

"It sounds like you're pretty open with your parents these days. At least they know about the boy."

"Well, they don't know everything."

"But they're telling you to get engaged and—"

"It's not like I said, 'Hey, I have a boyfriend.' I couldn't have done that."

"And his family's cool?"

"They're not crazy about their son marrying a Sunni, but other than that, they're cool."

"They're Shi'a?"

"Yep."

"Then you know I'm siding with them."

"Yeah, I remember your whole Karbala thing." The conversation hit another bump, and we couldn't face each other without words to say.

"Did I ever tell you that I'm F. Scott Fitzgerald?"

"I don't think so," she said. I failed to catch the sarcasm.

"Well, here's the thing—"

"Jesus, Mike! You've told me, like, a million times: You're F. Scott Fitzgerald reincarnated."

"'Reincarnation' might not be the proper term, but I'm him."

"I know you are, Mike."

"There's something to it, I think."

"I know."

"We have the same birthday, September 24. And he died on December 21, and I was born at 12:21 AM. Isn't that something?"

"It might be."

"In the Nation of Islam, you know, the Honorable Elijah Muhammad taught that both twelve and twenty-one are significant numbers."

"There you go."

"And in Scott's most famous short story, 'The Diamond as Big as the Ritz,' the protagonist's name was Unger—that's my dad's last name. In Zelda's novel *Save Me the Waltz*, who are the main characters? David and Alabama Knight. Knight is my mom's last name."

"Yep," she said, smiling patiently while my spiel ran its course.

"But the real shit is *Tender Is the Night*," I continued. "Dick Diver, you know, he has to ride a train from Buffalo to Virginia for his dad's funeral, which is what I'll have to do someday. Dick Diver also accidentally offends a character named Hosain and steals the Shah's car, and in the opening of the book, Scott describes the beach as a bright tan prayer rug. Tell me if that's not anything."

"No, Mike, it's something."

"You want to hear the kick in the ass?"

"Of course."

"*Tender Is the Night* ends in my hometown. Dick Diver moves to Geneva, New York."

"Yeah, I think you told me that."

"'A pleasant place,' it says, 'in the heart of the Finger Lakes.'"

"That's crazy, Mike."

"And Scott came from an Irish Catholic background; I came from an Irish Catholic background. Scott's mom had two babies die before he was born, and my mom had two miscarriages, so both our moms coddled us. My mom even told me that at one point she was going to name me Scott. And Fitzgerald's characters had dead or essentially absent fathers—how's that?"

"You must be him, then—except wasn't F. Scott a big alcoholic? You've never had a beer."

"Yeah, but that's part of it. Alcoholism destroyed Scott, and as a teenager I turned to a stern religion that completely forbade alcohol. So I never went to the parties and never experienced the dumb drunkenness of high school and college. It's like I'm spared from what made Fitzgerald a tragic figure."

"That sounds cool, actually."

"This time around, I'm doing it right."

Walking Fatima back to her house was accompanied by a growing sense of relief, since our tough last time was almost done. By the time we turned onto her street, awkward silences had become the norm. The real surprise came at times when actual words, even clumsy blurts of small talk that didn't mean anything, were said.

We stopped in front of her house. She said she'd miss me, but that we had to keep in touch. "Good luck with your Binghamton girl," she said.

"Good luck with your Shi'a boy."

Her arms wrapped around me one more time, for the story's sake.

Next I rode to Buffalo, where I knew a UB pharmacy major in the Endicott Complex. Samia was superpetite, with arms I could wrap my fingers around and no waist to speak of, a tiny Hyderabadi who could fly away in the breeze. Amazing Ayyub would have looked at a girl her size and said, *Shit, I'd split her in half like Zulfikar*, but girls like Samia made me want to take Ayyub's big gun and shoot him up his rectum.

I thought of that in the bus station restroom while waiting for her to come get me; someone had written, "Touch my junk" on the inside of the stall. It was the kind of thing Amazing Ayyub would write, but maybe it's what I'd write, too. Maybe it's what I'm writing now: "Touch my junk." Maybe it's Ben Majnun writing with his penis. One time I was standing at a Hobart College urinal, and saw that the grafitti in front of me read: "Don't look here for the joke. The joke is in your hand."

There were plenty of times when I felt like a joke and a loser, like when one of Basim's cousins wrote me after reading my punk book to say that the taqwacores objectified their women as much as conservative Muslims do: "What about that part where the guy has to educate a girl about her hymen? Are you saying that men know more about women's bodies than women?" No, I told her, that episode came from my real life: I really did have a Muslim girl whose mom kept her out of sex ed, and who was scared to get fingered. But when it came to the novel in general, maybe Basim's cousin wasn't wrong: I did have Muslimahs emailing me to say that the book had liberated them in ways they never would have expected, and had even convinced them to feel good about Islam, but still, I panicked that if they grew into graduate-level feminists, they'd see through it all.

In Alabama, a Pakistani-Bengali PhD student was waiting for me. I wrote something like twenty thousand words about her in another book, but that story was a long time ago. I wondered if she looked the same. Back then, she'd been a bony little girl, like all of these girls, and she'd still been a virgin, although she'd gone through miniature rebellions with boys.

I called her from the bus to tell her about my new road adventure, and said I'd be down in Birmingham at some point. We got to talking about our shared story with the unhappy ending, and she said she had something to tell me but wasn't sure if she should. I begged and whined until finally she came out with it: Back when I was really going hard on my books, it scared her.

"You were so into Master Fard that you became a different person."

"Do you still want to see me?"

"Of course I do. I just felt like I should say that."

"I'm not into Master Fard anymore."

"No, but you're into Clarence 13X, or you're into Hakim Bey. You're always into somebody or have some story going on." Sometimes it was Islamic anarchists; sometimes it was the Kominas or the Five Percenters or Parvez Musharraf's kid or whoever. The few girls who'd tell me how great it was that I could live my life with passion and do exactly what I wanted to do, I could never keep. What they called "passion" felt like drowning. Watch the guy struggle and panic in the water, and then say, "Wow, look at his passion; look at how passionate he is." Once girls realize that it's more like that, they're gone.

Alabama was a long way away. I got off the bus in Buffalo and called my UB girl, Samia. While waiting for her at the station, my feet got to itching so bad, I had to grind the heel of one boot into the toes of the other. Sometimes you can tell the status of a person's Islam by the condition of his feet—I wasn't making no wudhu five times a day.

Samia gave me a hug, and I apologized for my smell.

"How's the taqwacore scene going?" she asked in the car.

"It's good, I think. This white filmmaker was hanging around for a minute, wanting to do a documentary on Muslim punk bands. So I introduced her to the Kominas, and she asked them, 'What's it like being Muslim and knowing that you have these extremists in the community?' Can you believe that?"

"It's terrible. What'd the Kominas say?"

"Basim had a pretty good comeback: 'What's it like being white and knowing that there's Enron?'"

"Awesome."

"Meanwhile, Al Rukn's working on a novel, and his editor's a Gujrati girl who calls me a subcultural colonialist."

"What's that mean?"

"Colonialist of a subculture—I don't know."

"Maybe you are. You ever hear of Qur'an queens?"

"Are they another band?"

"No, my friend was telling me about them. It's a term in the gay Muslim community."

"So what are they—like, hafiz transvestites?" If anything, it had me thinking of the gay poet Rimbaud, who made his own translation of the Qur'an and ran guns in Africa.

"They're not even Muslim," she answered. "They're these white boys who go to the Al Fatiha conferences, hoping to hook up with 'exotic' brown men. Isn't that messed up?"

"I think I knew the hetero equivalent of that: this convert in Rochester who went to all the dinner parties and—"

"I think *you* are the hetero equivalent of that."

"Oh, whatever."

In her room, she got online and showed me the new poll at ProgressiveIslam.org:

"Michael Muhammad Knight . . ."
     converted to Islam for the desi girls
     went to Pakistan to learn how to say gulab jamun with authority

got into writing because the whole wrestling thing didn't
work out

challenged Ibrahim Hooper because he couldn't pin
Asma Hasan in a loser-stops-writing match

got into American Islam because his Arabic's no good

made up that whole Muslim punk thing, anyway

stays Muslim for the desi girls

"You want to see the results?" she asked, immediately clicking the option. Seventeen people had voted; "converted to
Islam for the desi girls" and "stays Muslim for the desi girls"
had taken most of the votes. Samia then asked what I had
been working on lately, so I offered to show her. I opened
an email attachment that I had sent to myself.

"Here you go."

"Progressive Islam vs. the Double-Dong Brothers," she
read. "Can I print this out?"

"Sure, but I can't be here when you read it. I'm going for
a walk."

My walk never took me out of her residence hall. It was
too much fun to go up and down each floor looking at dumb
dorm stuff on the walls, and the ways kids ornamented their
doors. After giving Samia enough time, I headed back to
her room. I had left her door cracked open so I could come
in without the card.

She smiled at me as though I needed a hug.

"Did you read it?"

"It was depressing, but I liked it."

"Thanks. Mohja Kahf's editing an anthology of American Muslim writers; that's my contribution."

"Your character was kind of unlikable, and Amazing Ayyub was completely beyond redemption. I hate him."

"That's probably appropriate."

"Because I know who you are and how you really feel, I'm not holding this story against you."

"Thanks."

"You're totally a teddy bear in real life, but when you write there's a certain sexism that comes out."

"Some people write about their bad parts," I told her.

"You're really hard on yourself. And when it comes to girls—like that onstage blow job scene in your novel, you know—you don't really look at their motivation. It's like girls only exist to provide or resolve conflict for your messed-up male characters."

"I could see that."

"It's the same sexist shit I found in Islam, and the same sexist shit in punk rock. Doesn't even matter what scene you're in—fuck all your scenes."

"Hakim Bey's not a patriarch," I told her. "He's queer."

"Hakim Bey writes about having sex with children."

We later went to Borders to see what new, comforting pap they had on the Islam shelf. Irshad Manji's *The Trouble with Islam* was out in paperback, diplomatically retitled *The Trouble with Islam Today*. Asra Nomani's *Standing Alone in Mecca* was now just *Standing Alone*. I'm in that book. On the same shelf stood Ibn Warraq's *Leaving*

Islam. I'm in there, too; my free contributor's copy from the publisher came addressed to Professor Knight. Then I saw Saleemah Abdul-Ghafur's *Living Islam Out Loud,* an anthology of writing by American Muslim women. I needed to slaughter all of them and get on that shelf—not in someone else's book, but in my own, with my name and messianic pose on the front cover, and some great blurb from John L. Esposito on the back: *Michael Muhammad Knight applies the principles and values of Islam to the realities of modern or postmodern life, taking up the challenge of reinterpretation and reform, critically and boldly addressing the major issues facing Muslims in the West.* Give me one from Michael Wolfe, too, to show off how I wrote with no guts and aimed to please, and let the inside jacket tell you how I'm blazing a trail for the Great New Huggable Islam. There was so much chaos and confusion in the ummah, maybe I could cash in if I played it right: get some royalties, go on NPR and scream (ripping off Ric Flair's victory speech from the 1992 Royal Rumble), "FOR ALL THE HIRSI ALIS, NOW IT'S MIKE KNIGHT, AND Y'ALL PAY HOMAGE TO THE MAN! WOOO!"

Samia asked what I thought of Irshad Manji. I gave the story of how I had once had dinner with Irshad, and she told me that she had never heard of the Five Percenters.

"That's kind of ridiculous," said Samia. "How's the Five Percenter book going, by the way?"

"It's done. I'm sending it around."

"What did they think of you writing about them?"

"Most have been great about it. I mean they want to know where you're coming from and what you're planning to do with them, but once you've been to enough parliaments and know enough people, and show that you've been on the inside of the cipher for a while now . . ."

"Didn't they even give you a Five Percenter name?"

"Yeah, I'm Azreal Wisdom."

"That's so cool. They like you."

I didn't tell her that in Harlem I'd still build like a Five Percenter and really was Azreal Wisdom, that I'd never treated my time with them as any kind of tourism or wormy journalist caper. But later, she took me to see the new movie about Truman Capote, which had me spending the rest of the night asking myself if I had in fact Capoted the Five Percenters. We later held each other in her bed, where I thought about her helping to graft me back into the Original Man. Instead we just talked.

It came up in conversation that I had once planned to start a wrestling federation in Egypt and had an Egyptian championship belt custom-made for it.

"Doesn't that plan seem a little out of touch with reality?"

"Yeah, I guess it does."

"But it didn't seem that way back when you were doing it, when you really had your heart in it?"

"No, it didn't."

"That's totally a manic symptom. Do you go through that a lot?"

"Here and there."

"And do you get depressed, too?"

"It all balances out."

"You're manic-depressive, Azreal Wisdom." She noticed the scar on my head. I showed her the other one by my right eye.

"They used forceps in my delivery," I told her, knowing that she'd have fun with that.

"You probably have frontal-lobe damage," she said. I kissed her on the forehead and we fell asleep.

The next day, I called Al Rukn in New York City. He told me that I had missed the launch party of the Pakistani American magazine *Chowrangi*. Al Rukn had gone to the party with Shahjehan Khan, and they'd both gotten drunk off their ass. While Al Rukn went on angry rants and made belligerent attempts at hitting on the desi girls, a happy-drunk Shahj went up to Mike Myers, delivered the succinct proclamation "Muslim punk rock!" and handed him a CD of Kominas demos. "Thanks," said Austin Powers, and then the sloshed Komina disappeared back into the party.

I took a bus to the city and stood with Al Rukn and Shahjehan outside a bar in Brooklyn where Shahj's friends were playing. Shahj had come to Brooklyn with no money and turned Al Rukn's loft into a taqwacore halfway house, crashing for a week or so and eating all of his food. Al Rukn and Shahjehan had been building on ideas for the upcoming Kominas video, which Al Rukn was slated to direct, and one of them told me about some kafr who thought that they should have bikini-clad girls in leather burqa tops.

Shahjehan told me that the day after the *Chowrangi* party, his friend at the new MTV Desi channel had taken him on a tour of the MTV studios. "See that?" I cried in front of the bar. "See how it starts, Shahj? Let me tell you what's going to happen . . ." Then I delivered an impromptu sidewalk performance of the whole Amazing Ayyub story in which a taqwacore band goes pop and Ayyub has to kill them. "And you die in it, too, Shahjehan; you go to Utah to fight zombies created by Hamza Yusuf, and the zombies kill you, and Basim cremates you so that you don't turn into a zombie yourself, and then Hamza Yusuf takes on the form of a female jinn to give Amazing Ayyub a hand job because he's trying to find the Kominas!" Shahj and Al Rukn got a kick out of the show, so I kept on going. I promised them that I knew the secret of the white male convert, that I could dig deep into that brain and pull out all of its secret ugliness, announced my plans for literary autodecapitation, and delivered a rough version of Rabeya's final monologue. "You have to write it out," said Al Rukn, "and see it through to the end." That night I could have crashed at Al Rukn's taqwacore loft, but I went to Penn Station instead and waited six hours to get on a Greyhound to New Jersey.

Most of my Sufi quotes came from this kind of flaky girl Noorjahan, who went to Drew University in Madison and filled her notebooks with wise words from famous shaykhs and saints. She was the one who told me that Rumi said something about the apostates being the ones who love Allah the most, which I liked; at least it could have been Rumi—she wasn't sure. I returned the favor by telling her that according to al-Ash'ari, there were six female prophets: Eve, Sarah, Yukabid (the mother of Moses), Hagar, Asiya, and Maryam.

Noorjahan picked me up at the bus station and took me back to her dorm. On the door to her room she had one of those washable message boards with no messages, only another quote:

> *I am looking for Serif.*
> *I am not looking for Allah.*
> —Serif

She offered me part of a leftover sandwich, but all I cared about was getting my shoes off and stretching out on her bed. While I closed my eyes and tried to forget about the buses, she sat at her desk and played around on her computer. I heard the sounds of her briefly IMing someone.

"I still have your quote that you gave me," she said, calling my attention to a pink Post-it note stuck on the top shelf of her standard-issue dorm desk.

"What quote was that?"

"'By the sweet breath of Allah, all life is bound to one; so if you touch a fiber of a living thing, you send a thrill from the center to the outer bounds of life'—Noble Drew Ali."

"Do you know who he is yet?"

"He was like . . . who's that guy you're into, again?"

"Don't worry about it."

"I've been getting into the Jerrahis. You ever look into them? They have shaykhas; that's pretty cool."

"What's a shaykha?"

"Like a woman shaykh."

"Oh, right." I looked over and saw that she was now on the Jerrahi Order's website.

"Do you want to see the Jerrahis' translation of Al Fatiha?"

"Read it to me."

"It's really cool; there's no mention of punishment or anger. Wait a minute . . . okay, here it is: I take refuge with Allah the All-Merciful from the principle of rebellion and negativity . . . in the name of Allah Most High who is Tenderly Compassionate, Infinitely Merciful, perfect praise flows to Allah alone, Lover and Sustainer of all Worlds, most intimately called Rahman and Rahim, presiding magnificently over the Day of Divine Awakening. O Lord, we worship only You and rely upon You alone. Reveal Your Direct Path, the mystic way of those who, through Your Mercy, have received and truly assimilated Your sublime guidance, those who never wander from the spiritual path and therefore never experience Your Awesome Correction."

"Sounds like they took some creative license."

Later that night, as Noorjahan drove us to the prayer-rug beach, I thought of Ibn 'Arabi's saying that nobody really worships Allah, since Allah is too unknowable to worship, so deep down we're only worshipping ourselves. It was a Five Percenter in Brooklyn who told me that. The things this girl imagined as Allah were really her own personality traits. I looked at my own Allah, who booked these angles like His personal wrestling federation, pushing and burying champions and pulling swerve heel-turns to keep the marks interested, doing it only for entertaining stories, sometimes involving Himself as a character, too—the Vince McMahon of the Universe—and then it scared me to think of the people who love for Allah to be mean and wrathful, the ones who really get off on the idea of other people burning forever.

She wanted to swim, but I said it was too cold. She turned her back to the water, pulled off her shirt and laid it on the concrete, showing her wiry little body and her black bra. She took off her jeans standing up. Her underwear was black, too. She walked into the water, going slow until it reached her knees, then lunged forward and submerged for a second, blasting back to the surface as though fired from a cannon.

"*Shit!*" she screamed, pushing wet hair from her eyes. I stripped down to blue plaid boxers and went in ankle deep. My legs could handle cold from having walked around Buffalo through a few Decembers wearing shorts. Twenty feet away, Noorjahan sent herself under again and jumped back up, moonlight shining on her body. She reached behind her head, grabbed her long hair with both hands, and wrung it out. Then she called me a sorry excuse for a Sufi.

"WHAT'S THIS HAVE TO DO WITH SUFISM?" I

yelled from the bottom of my lungs, so she would hear over the waves.

"RUWAYN BIN AHMAD SAID, 'SUFISM CONSISTS OF ABANDONING ONESELF TO ALLAH IN ACCORDANCE WITH WHAT ALLAH WILLS!"

"SO ALLAH WILLS FOR ME TO FREEZE OFF MY NUTS?"

"AS ABU SAID PUT IT: 'BEING A SUFI IS TO PUT AWAY WHAT IS IN YOUR HEAD—IMAGINED TRUTHS, PRECONCEPTIONS, CONDITIONING—AND FACE WHAT MAY HAPPEN TO YOU!" That was a good one, I thought, but I had some, too.

"ABU MUHAMMAD AL-JARIRI," I yelled, "SAID THAT 'SUFISM CONSISTS OF ENTERING EVERY EXALTED QUALITY AND LEAVING BEHIND EVERY DESPICABLE QUALITY!' SO TELL ME WHAT'S EXALTED HERE!"

"SAMNUN SAID, 'SUFISM IS THAT YOU SHOULD NOT POSSESS ANYTHING, NOR SHOULD ANYTHING POSSESS YOU!'" Noorjahan looked at the water, leaned back, and let a wave knock her down. "HERE YOU GO," she added, back on her feet. "AMR BIN UTHMAN AL-MAKKI SAID, 'SUFISM IS THAT EACH MOMENT SHOULD BE IN ACCORD WITH WHAT IS MOST APPROPRIATE AT THAT MOMENT!' SO YOU'RE HERE AND STANDING BALLS DEEP IN THE ATLANTIC—WHAT CAN YOU DO?" I hesitated, tensed up, threw myself down, and launched back up, screaming threats and curses at the water. Noorjahan cheered. I spit a few times, having forgotten that it was saltwater.

Once we were out of the ocean, we realized the flaws of our plan. There wasn't much we could do about wet feet on a sandy beach without totally crudding up our towels. After putting on my pants, I realized that a grain of sand is really just a tiny, sharp rock. I had a dozen tiny, sharp rocks hiding on the hairs of each leg, scratching with every step. And I still had wet boxers on.

"I feel a diaper rash coming on," I said in Noorjahan's car, sitting on a towel. She drove us back to her school, and I stole a slice of someone's pizza from the dorm's communal refrigerator. Noorjahan called me a scumbag and added that according to Ma'ruf of Baghdad, Sufism means "to grasp the verities and renounce that which is in the hands of Allah's creatures." I was too busy with my slice to answer.

I finished my shower first and waited on her bed. She came in, turned off the light, and joined me.

"Sorry you have all this wet hair in your face now."

"That's fine."

"Do you really have a thing for desi girls?"

"I don't think I do."

"No, you do, you do. But it's okay. I don't think you're one of *those* guys, necessarily—white guys who convert and then go after immigrants' daughters are usually hardcore sexist assholes." Then there was the special dilemma white female converts faced: Because white male converts were patriarchs in denial, they wanted traditional brown girls, and because black male converts were cultural nationalists, they wanted black women. The only Muslims who wanted white women were Arab men, and even the liberal, feministic Arab men were too culturally fucked to deal with Westernized women.

"So what am I, then?"

"You're a Reese's White Chocolate Peanut Butter Cup," she replied.

"Let me guess . . ."

"White on the outside and brown on the inside."

"Brilliant."

"You're a nice rebel, but you know desi girls can't end up with you. *They* know they can't end up with you. No matter how cool or romantic they think it is, in the end they'll always take the safer bet. And that really hurts you, but still, you set yourself up to go through it again and again, since you like to keep on killing yourself."

"Yeah, it's a good time."

"So you're all right. Maybe it's working-class rage with you, at least some of it, since they're always on their way to grad school. Or maybe it's Progressive-Muslim rage." F. Scott Fitzgerald had working-class rage ("Rich girls don't marry poor boys, Jay Gatsby"), but I wasn't even sure if Scott himself really knew it. Instead of wanting to kill the rich, he wanted to *be* them; he longed to sneak into the party and fool everyone into thinking he belonged there.

"The Progressives have no rage," I said.

"All right." She turned back around. "Look at you," she said in a fake South Asian accent, "in the Muslim sister's bed—this is very very bad."

"You're not my sister." Then she didn't say anything for a long time.

"You know, it goes the other way, too."

"What goes the other way?" I asked.

"Everyone loves a convert. You didn't *have* to be Muslim; you could have been at the high school keggers; you could have had girlfriends, but instead you chose the deen. And not only did you embrace Islam all on your own, but you knew more than the kids who had been born and raised in it. I'm sure the girls at the masjid found you interesting."

"It was more the uncles. They thought I'd run the mosque someday."

"You could have been Hamza Yusuf, you know that?"

"Sure."

"Where are you going to end up?"

"There's this guy Karamustafa in St. Louis who's a professor. I think I'll camp outside his house."

"I meant more internally."

"I don't know. I think I have to figure out what I really believe."

"Why?"

"Maybe I've been into this whole heresy thing to avoid actually having an idea about Islam that I want to stand up for."

"So now you feel like you have to figure it out?"

"Have to sometime."

"Hujari said, 'A path has no value once you've arrived.' And Abd al-Kader said, 'The search has no final finding. Knowledge of Allah is without end.'"

"Imam Shafi said that if you became a Sufi at Fajr time, you'd be an idiot by Zuhr."

"JESUS CHRIST, YOU'RE SUCH A DICK!" She punched me in the arm and had me scared for a second, but then said she was kidding. We slept in the same bed, but that was all; sometimes I had my arm around her, and sometimes I got erections that went unacknowledged and died on their own.

Then I had only one girl left: a failed fairy tale in Alabama, the Pakistani-Bengali future doctor whose parents called me John Walker Lindh, the rich-girls-don't-marry-poor-boys one who ripped me apart a few times and then rebuilt me, just to do it again. I called her during my ride home and made up a story about being stuck in Michigan.

"Then we're probably never going to see each other again," she said.

"Maybe we will."

"We shouldn't if you get another Muslim girlfriend."

"I guess not."

"Well, you know we would have ruined each other's lives, anyway."

"You wouldn't have been happy," I told her. "You would have resented me."

"You'd hate me," she answered. "I'd kill your writing, I know it."

"When I finally get back home, I'll be working on a new novel."

"Really? What's it about?"

"I'm going to have this Muslimah who wants to join the rodeo, but her parents won't let her because she's a girl. So she secretly rides in the rodeo anyway and somehow ends up proving that you can ride in the rodeo and still be a Muslim woman, living your lipstick jihad out loud."

"That doesn't sound like something you'd write."

"I could get it published, though. I'm calling it *Buffalo Tandoori*."

"It won't be any good."

"Her best friend's going to be a gay Jewish boy who dies in 9/11, and she'll dedicate her rodeo trophy to him."

"That sounds terrible."

After losing my cell phone signal, I just looked out the bus window and pictured my broken carcass hobbling back to the ring, climbing up the cage again, and receiving a choke-slam through the roof.

THE MAIN EVENT

 I HAD MY Michael Muhammad Knight character still at the Herman Street house so that Amazing Ayyub could have a place to go once he hit town. After arriving at the Greyhound station, Ayyub trudged through downtown and then the whole way up Elmwood Avenue. As he neared the state-college campus, he decided to shake off his invisiblity and started getting strange looks for his gun. In front of Jim's Steak-Out, he found two desi punks with a brand-new bike and a shopping cart that had been suped up with ropes and duct tape holding baskets and buckets along the sides—a hobo dream machine. The older of the two might have been around Ayyub's age, but it was hard to say, since bums age at their own rate. His beard was scriggle-scraggle. He wore a blue T-shirt with the Superman logo, and frayed khaki shorts that revealed dried blood and open sores on his calves. The younger looked nineteen or twenty and seemed to have not been a bum for very long; he was still too clean and not yet relaxed within the role. His shiny bike looked like the last relic of a better life he'd once known.

"Don't shoot!" the older one joked to Ayyub, throwing his arms in the air. Ayyub didn't get the joke until he remembered his gun. The guy asked Ayyub for money, and Ayyub gave the pair his last $5, knowing that he'd be all right once he made it to Herman Street.

The older bum explained to Amazing Ayyub that the younger one was homeless only because he couldn't handle his girlfriend leaving him. This kid had gambled everything on his heart and lost, then found himself at the city mission, where the older one had discovered him, and they'd formed a tag team.

"I know the city mission," said Ayyub, and the dude's face beamed as though they shared a mutual friend. "Camp Fun, I used to call it. They won't let you dump in private because they think we're all on drugs."

"You said it!"

"I got a hand job there one time," said Ayyub.

"Look at this kid," said the older bum, putting his arm around his buddy. "We're gonna start a taqwacore band, me and him. I don't know what we're calling it yet."

"I was in a taqwa band," replied Ayyub, puffing out his chest so they could see his homemade shirt. "The Submumins."

"That's beautiful. We're gonna start a band, aren't we?" The bum still had his arm around the kid, told him he was good shit and didn't need that girl anyway—that bitch, she'd figure out someday what she had missed out on—but the kid just looked at the sidewalk, not knowing what to do. The older one explained to Amazing Ayyub that the younger one had been drinking a lot of vodka and doing other stuff, but nobody had any idea what—tranquilizers, maybe, or acid. Ayyub looked at the kid's sad eyes to see if they were right. Not only were they not right, they were *wrong*, and in forty years or so they'd be even sadder.

The older one then asked the younger one if he could borrow his bike "for just a minute, just to go down the block and come right back," and it turned into a begging show, with the kid saying he didn't know and his partner laying down promises, offering his cart and all that it contained as collateral, but the kid didn't want the cart or *anything* it contained; he was just worried about his bike. After enough haggling, though, he gave in and let Superman ride away, ass hovering high above the seat.

"You're a good friend for him," said Amazing Ayyub.

"He looks out for me, too," said the kid. I wished Amazing Ayyub knew that girl Noorjahan; she would have told him how Ibrahim Khawas said that poverty is a robe of honor, cloak of apostles and mantle of the upright, and Ayyub could have relayed the words to this rookie vagrant. Then a white Buff State boy came out of We Never Close with a tall can of beer, pouring it into his hands and then slapping it on his neck, as if it were cologne.

"What the fuck are you doing?" Ayyub asked.

"Getting ready for the Elmwood Avenue girls!" the white boy replied, swaggering over to two by the curb. "Helloooo, ladies." They made apprehensive eye contact and turned away. "What's your names?" he asked. Neither answered. "I'M FUCKIN' WASTED RIGHT NOW!" he screamed. Beer still in hand, he then ran across the street to where the liquor store had stacked up a pile of empty cardboard boxes for garbage pickup, and sent them flying with a kick before working a decent faux-drunk fall. He managed to hold on to his beer and keep it upright until he hit the ground, at which point the can got away and emptied itself onto the street.

"Yeah," said one of the girls. "That's what we like to see."

"Damn!" said a guy to his cell phone. "This drunk asshole hit his head." Everyone went on their way, leaving just the white boy, Amazing Ayyub, and the younger desi punk.

"Was it a decent bump?" the white kid asked.

"Looked like a concussion to me," Ayyub answered.

"I can play a pretty good Buff State drunk. When they come back through here, those girls'll be up on my shit."

"Hell yeah."

"You wouldn't even believe this, but I just got kicked out of Porter Hall! You know Porter Hall? Over there, at the school?"

"I know Porter Hall," said Ayyub.

"Well, I got fuckin' . . . busted for weed."

"And they kicked you out?"

"I'm as good as kicked out, yo—I got fuckin' thrown out of Perry already for setting my ramen noodles on fire and tossin' them out the window, so they moved me to Porter, and now you have this shit."

"You're like the sacred victim, bro."

"Yeah," said the white boy, resigned to his fate. "Yo, that's a big fuckin' gun you got. You could shoot some big dogs with that gun."

"You could shoot a lot of things with this gun," said Ayyub.

"Right on."

While the desi bum stayed behind, waiting for his bike to return, Amazing Ayyub and the white kid walked together down Elmwood to the art museum and contemplated ways of making it onto the roof. The kid told Amazing Ayyub that he used to sell LSD until that one time he got stabbed. "Damn," said Ayyub. They found a ledge, Ayyub tossed up his gun and bag of clothes and climbed after them, and the two punks wandered around on one of the lower levels, walking by windows, pretending to be art thieves. Ayyub and his big gun crept up to windows and passed them with superspy poses, as if he were some elite assassin, which he'd actually be in a day or two.

"Shit, man," said the kid. "I'm gonna fall off this shit and break my neck." Across Elmwood from the art museum stood Buffalo State's Rockwell Hall. Amazing Ayyub told the kid that he used to piss on those pillars. The kid laughed. "You went to Buff State?" he asked.

"I have two degrees," announced Ayyub, "Criminal justice and sociology, and I was homeless all five years." Back when Amazing Ayyub had worked overnights at Wal-Mart, his boss had always given him shit: "Hey, Ayyub, I always wanted to see a cop clean a toilet . . . Hey, Ayyub, I always wondered how a sociologist would mop the floor."

"One time," Ayyub told the kid, "I lived the whole summer in the North Wing and nobody knew."

"How'd you manage that?"

"I just carried it all with me, bro. I had my clothes in a garbage bag like this one, and when I had to go somewhere I'd take it and prop the door with a rock so I could get back in."

"That's a lifestyle," said the kid. "You ever get caught?"

"No way." Back in those days, Amazing Ayyub had slept naked but worn a ski mask in case someone discovered him. Ayyub liked to joke about it: *They would have made us stand in a cock lineup*, he'd say. *Sir, is that the cock of the man you found sleeping in the North Wing? Ha-ha.*

This kid with Amazing Ayyub could have been an Adept of the Third Paradise or just another Buffalo State jackass. He was hungry for something, though perhaps only in the dumb, eighteen-year-old, quixotic nonstarter sense: half wanting hikmah but never in any serious way; climbing on an art museum and not knowing shit about anything; restless to figure it out but yearning at one moment to bitch rides across the country and end up in Alaska, and the next wanting only to get with a female that he knew in Porter.

"You ever fuck a black girl?" the kid asked.

"Sure."

"What's it like?"

"They're all pink on the inside." Then the kid remembered that instead of trespassing at the Albright-Knox, he could be over in Porter Hall, trying to talk to the girl in mind, so he said goodbye to Ayyub and ran off. Ayyub hung out by himself for a while and then realized that he still had a lot of walking to do. He got back to his journey, hiking dangerously on the shoulder of the 198 and later the 33 as tractor-trailers rattled by and jerkoffs yelled at him from their cars. No one seemed to think that his unrealistically large machine gun was indeed a functioning firearm capable of blowing baseball-size holes through their doors. Ayyub never even thought to render himself invisible again; it would have been a bad idea on those busy highways. His feet hurt and made him remember that sorry limp he had developed walking from Herman Street to Wal-Mart and back all the time for his overnight janitor's job. Ayyub suffered his way to Michael Muhammad Knight's house, went to the backyard, and found the abandoned car. He opened the door and crawled in, and it actually felt like home. His old spit-out date pits were even still in the passenger seat, and the driver's seat was still pushed back from the last time he'd slept there, however long ago that was. Ayyub pulled off his boots, and they smelled so bad that he had to leave them outside the car with his gun. He closed the door behind him, threw Yusuf Islam's dad's clothes in the back-seat, to be forgotten forever, and looked at the Submumins shirt he had on—the way Amazing Ayyub did things, an acquired shirt could be the only evidence for a whole chapter of his life. *The Submumins*, he thought. *The Submumins are a real thing that really happened somewhere.* Ayyub took off the shirt, closed his eyes, and knocked out.

The next morning, Michael Muhammad Knight opened the door, causing Ayyub to immediately snap awake and jerk up his body with his fists cocked.

"He returns," said the author. "Ayyub, are you insane? What's with this obscene weapon out here?"

"I'm on a mission, bro."

"What do you mean, you're on a mission? I thought you were on a mission in California, with Rabeya."

"She's gone, and she might have blown Matt Damon's head off."

"Good lord, Ayyub."

"That girl gave me the chills anyway."

"I know what you mean," said the author. "Rabeya reveals me as completely transparent."

"Hell yeah, brother."

"Sees right through me." Michael Muhammad Knight swept the date pits off the passenger seat and got in the car with him.

"You know what *you* need, Michael?"

"What's that, Ayyub?"

"A shit-jerk."

"A shit-jerk?"

"A shit-jerk, bro. We go get an *Artvoice*, and in the back they have all those ads for girls that wack you off for money."

"Is that really what I need?"

"It's not what you *don't* need, Michael."

They climbed out of the dead car, walked ten feet to the author's Buick, and drove to Elmwood Avenue to find the new *Artvoice*. Two-For-One Pizza had a stack of them. Amazing Ayyub ordered a slice, and when it came out on its paper plate, he buried the thing under a hill of garlic powder.

"THAT'S ENOUGH!" yelled the accented old pizza man.

"I thought it was free," said Ayyub.

"YOU DO THIS EVERY TIME! NO MORE!" Michael Muhammad Knight and Amazing Ayyub went outside and sat on the curb. The author thought about his favorite character's shitty life, and how maybe it made him feel better to win these little battles, just to put himself over for once. Ayyub spread the *Artvoice* out on the street in front of him and flipped to the ads in back while chewing.

"Here's one," he said with his mouth full. "Her name's Savannah, and she'll jerk you off good, brother. Get out all your troubles; don't you worry about a thing." Ayyub took the author's cell phone and called her, sticking a greasy finger in his ear to block out the sounds of Elmwood life. Michael Muhammad Knight heard only Ayyub's side of the conversation: What did she look like, how tall was she, what were her rates, could he tip . . .

Then Ayyub asked, "What's that entail?" and Michael Muhammad Knight tried hard not to laugh—first wondering what had provoked the question, then loving that Amazing Ayyub would try to come off as a square businessman with a word like "entail." Ayyub asked if she took in calls, apparently got the right answer, and said he'd be right over. "Sounds good," he said, handing the author back his phone with pizza junk on it. "What'd I tell you, bro? You stick with Ayyub, he'll take care of everything." They walked back to the car.

"It's so fuckin' early," moaned Michael Muhammad Knight in the driver's seat, keys still in Ayyub's pocket. "Let me close my eyes for a minute."

"Okay, bro." They both reclined their seats. Michael Muhammad Knight pulled his blanket up from the backseat and they shared it. "What's today's mathematics?" asked Ayyub. In the Five Percenters' system of Supreme Mathematics, each number carried a unique attribute, used by Gods to employ figures such as the day's date as rhetorical instruments.

"Knowledge Born," said the author. "Knowledge, you know, Knowledge is the foundation—that's where it all starts. That's why one is Knowledge. And nine is Born because it takes that many months for a fetus to develop in the womb. So when you have Knowledge and you make it Born, that means you're manifesting your Knowledge out there in the world."

"That's peace," Ayyub replied.

"I talk to some Gods in Pittsburgh," said the author.

"This one God, he knows a God out in California who built with John Walker Lindh back in the day."

"Who's that?"

"The so-called American Taliban—you know, that kid they found in Afghanistan. That's some shit, isn't it? He dabbled in the Five Percent before going balls-out Sunni."

"Like the opposite of you," said Amazing Ayyub.

Some time later, they were woken up by a police officer standing on Michael Muhammad Knight's side of the car.

COP: What are you guys doing in there?

MICHAEL MUHAMMAD KNIGHT: Oh, we must have fallen asleep.

COP: Can I see your IDs?

MICHAEL MUHAMMAD KNIGHT (handing over his driver's license): Here.

AMAZING AYYUB: Why do you want to see my ID?

COP: Just let me see it.

AMAZING AYYUB: I'm not doing anything wrong.

COP (to Michael Muhammad Knight): You better tell your friend here to give me his ID.

MICHAEL MUHAMMAD KNIGHT: Ayyub, man. Come on.

AMAZING AYYUB: We're not doing anything wrong, bro. Why's he want to see my ID?

COP: It's two guys lying back in a car, you know? You got this blanket over you, you've got your shirt off—

AMAZING AYYUB: We're not fuckin' homos!

The cop called for backup. Amazing Ayyub and Michael Muhammad Knight were asked to step outside, and Ayyub finally coughed up his only ID—a crumpled New York State handgun permit—but yelled and waved his hands and insisted that he wasn't a homo. The first officer asked Michael Muhammad Knight if he actually knew Ayyub or if they had just met—what the hell did that mean? Eventually Michael Muhammad Knight and Amazing Ayyub got their IDs back, and the cops let them drive away.

AMAZING AYYUB: I showed them.

MICHAEL MUHAMMAD KNIGHT: What did you show them, exactly?

AMAZING AYYUB: They respect me now.

MICHAEL MUHAMMAD KNIGHT: How do you figure?

AMAZING AYYUB: : I wasn't afraid.

MICHAEL MUHAMMAD KNIGHT: Amazing Ayyub, you're a madman. You know that, right? You're completely unequipped to deal with society.

AMAZING AYYUB: You're right, Michael. I'm sorry.

MICHAEL MUHAMMAD KNIGHT: It's all right, Ayyub-jaan. Maybe you're the spiritual pole of your time.

If not this taqwa skin, who was it?

"How'd you get so strong, Amazing Ayyub?" asked Michael Muhammad Knight with a glance at Ayyub's veiny forearm. "You never eat anything."

"Workin' for Budweiser in Newburgh, loading kegs on trucks."

"I could see you doing that."

"Those kegs weigh eighty-five pounds a pop, and they don't want any late deliveries. You gotta load that shit up."

"How long were you down in Newburgh?"

"I wish you could have seen my dog," said Ayyub, suddenly energetic, ignoring the author's question. "My dog was a crazy dog, but it's my fault. I made him crazy."

"How'd you make him crazy?"

"When he was a puppy, I used to soak a rag in steak juice and then smack him in the face with it. From then on, he was wacked out."

"That'll do it."

"You remember me, Michael? Like, when I lived in Buffalo all the time?"

"Yeah, Amazing Ayyub, I remember."

Ayyub showed Michael Muhammad Knight the way to the *Artvoice* slut's house. The author looked at the car clock and realized that they had slept for two hours, so Ayyub called her again and made sure it was still okay to come over. She said sure, and he told Michael Muhammad Knight the address.

"See, bro?" Ayyub said, smiling. "She's not mad. We're the customer—*you're* the customer. The customer is always right, Michael. The customer is always about to get his SHIT JERKED, YEEEE-HEE-HEE!" Michael Muhammad Knight pulled up to the curb in front of her house. "TIME FOR THE JERKING OF THE SHIT!"

"Amazing Ayyub, once we get out of the car, I want you to be a human being."

"Okay, bro. Don't you worry about a thing."

They walked up to the door, and the author knocked. Amazing Ayyub couldn't stop giggling. A girl who looked maybe two tiers below Vivid Video quality came to the front porch and through the screen door asked them what they wanted.

"Are you Savannah?" asked Amazing Ayyub.

"No, I'm her sister. Savannah's not here."

"Oh. Okay." Amazing Ayyub and Michael Muhammad Knight walked back to the car. "That's some bullshit," Ayyub snapped. "That was fuckin' Savannah—I know it. That dirty whore."

"Why'd she lie?"

"Bet she was freaked out by there being two of us."

"Or just one of you . . . for Christ's sake, Ayyub, you don't even have a shirt on."

"Fuck it, bro. There's plenty of fish in the sea, right?"

"Right, Amazing Ayyub."

"Right. There's plenty of fish in the sea, plenty of whores in Buffalo." Amazing Ayyub's next course of action was to drive Michael Muhammad Knight to a massage parlor down by the Buffalo death strip of abandoned factories and warehouses. The author remembered an ancient battlefield in that part of town: the adult-video store and its parking lot where Ayyub had waged war against the Double-Dong Brothers.

"Here we go," said Ayyub: "the shit-jerk parlor. These girls'll shake your shit for ten bucks." It was just a grimy house with a neon Massage sign in the window, but the sign was off and it didn't seem like anyone was inside.

"Don't you worry about a thing," said Ayyub. "There's plenty of whores in Buffalo; we've got a thriving sex industry here—how do you think anyone affords nice cars in Buffalo? Sex industry, brother."

Shit-jerkings.

"Looks closed," said Michael Muhammad Knight.

"FUCK!" Ayyub shrieked. "All I wanted was for you to get your dingaling spanked!"

"Thanks, Amazing Ayyub."

"Pull in here," Ayyub said, gesturing to the neighboring bank's parking lot. Amazing Ayyub jumped out of the car and ran behind the parlor, hoisting up a Dumpster lid to reveal clear plastic garbage bags soaked with old rain. "Probably porn in here," he whispered, holding the lid up with both hands.

"Ayyub, man—"

"Dude, dude, bro, listen—if we find a used condom, we can shut this place down."

"Do we need to shut this place down?"

"Yeah, Michael. They're no good, these places. They fuck with your mind. Aoudhu billah, let's get out of here."

"Where you want to go?"

"Let's go to Wegmans and call Savannah from a payphone so she doesn't know that it's us—dammit, Michael! What's wrong with Buffalo that I can't even get my friend a decent shit-jerk? No wonder this town's falling apart."

Savannah wouldn't answer her phone, so they drove back to the shit-jerk parlor and found the place open. Inside it looked like a waiting room, much like that of a doctor's office, except dimly lit and dingy, and instead of *People* or *Newsweek*, the coffee table offered a newsprint directory of strip clubs, adult stores, escort services, and massage parlors throughout the Niagara region. "My friend needs one of your best massagers," said Amazing Ayyub. The fifty-year-old pervert of a manager, with a long comb-over, a three-day beard, and a sloppy, wide-collared shirt, looked Ayyub up and down.

"You got a shirt?"

"I left it at home."

He asked Amazing Ayyub for $35. Ayyub slapped it down, and the manager emerged from behind the counter in his bare feet to walk the author down the hall. Michael Muhammad Knight noticed an open bathroom with a shower.

"Am I supposed to shower first?" he asked.

"You can if you want. Then, when you're done, take this room right here." So Michael Muhammad Knight went in, rinsed off (they had no soap) under the shower's weak little dribble, got dressed, and walked five feet to the massage room, where he took his clothes off again and sat on the table. He played with himself just to get long for when the girl came in. He waited and waited while his penis went long and short a few times. After fifteen minutes, the creepy manager opened the door and told the naked author that his girl had gotten sick and had had to go home. The manager apologized profusely and gave Michael Muhammad Knight two vouchers, each good for $5 off his next hand job. "We should be open again at five," said the manager. "Come back then. We'll have a redhead."

"That's some bullshit," whined Amazing Ayyub in the car. "Sick, my ass—that girl had a coke fit."

"Really?"

"I saw her, bro. Eighteen years old, skinny from all the coke and smack she's doing. She yelled at the shady guy and went off about somethin' crazy—who the fuck knows? She flipped her sex-worker lid."

"A coke fit, damn."

"They're all on coke, bro."

"You think so?"

"Why else would they be jerking shit for a living?"

They drove back to Herman Street. "You know, Michael," said Amazing Ayyub, "I hate cops, but I think I'm gonna be one soon."

"What's with that?" asked Michael Muhammad Knight.

"Time to flip the see-saw."

"I hear you."

"Bro, the Shi'as have always been on the bottom."

"I know, Amazing Ayyub."

"The Sixth Imam said it's okay for you to lie about being a Shi'a if it'd save your life."

"How do you feel about that?"

"I'd let them gun me down, though. I'd just fuckin' take it."

"You've got heart, I'll give you that."

"You think so?"

"I've never known anyone who could live like you."

"A-plus, bro. You know, Michael, I could be a corrections officer over at Attica. Seventeen dollars an hour, just to start."

The Eighth Imam said that cleanliness was a badge of the prophets, but there were no prophets at 376 Herman Street, and the place still smelled like stale, dirty clothes and ancient Ayyub sperm crust. Besides, the Eighth Imam had been poisoned by Mamoon the Abbasid. Michael Muhammad Knight collapsed onto his mattress and napped long enough for Amazing Ayyub to go back into the world and gather up some money.

Shortly after five, Ayyub woke him up by slapping him in the face with a wad of bills.

"Where'd that come from?" groaned the author. "You mow some lawns?"

"Mow some lawns? What are you talking about? Get up!"

"Ayyub, man—"

"I wouldn't even be mowing that lady's lawn, anyway. She saw me pissing on her tulips, remember?"

"Yeah, I think so."

"She got all mad, so I put a turd in her mailbox."

"Why'd you even do that, Amazing Ayyub?"

"Don't worry about it, Michael. We need to go get a whore."

"Why's it so important to get a whore?"

"'Cause it's our last night, brother." Michael Muhammad Knight wasn't sure what that meant, but it sounded right enough.

"Are we going back to the shit-jerk parlor?"

"Never, bro. That place was skeevy. We're going to Niagara Falls; they'll take good care of you up there."

Michael Muhammad Knight went through his pile of clothes and fished out a wrinkled button-up shirt for himself. Amazing Ayyub wore one of Yusuf Islam's dad's shirts. At the border, Ayyub told the border cop that their reason for visiting Canada was to see some naked girls. "Can you believe it?" he whispered to the author while the customs cop looked over his ID. "New York state says I can own a handgun!" They crossed into Canada, and Amazing Ayyub navigated the author down Lundy's Lane, stopping at the money exchange before arriving at a pink building draped in so much neon light, it couldn't have been anything but a strip club or a casino. "How do I look?" Ayyub asked the author.

"You look good," the author replied, though Ayyub could never look natural or comfortable in one of those shirts. If anything, he looked more like a creep for trying to disguise himself.

Inside they claimed a table and watched the strippers, each girl doing two onstage dances, until Michael Muhammad Knight saw the one he wanted: She called herself Sahara. After watching her dance to two Ludacris songs, he approached her at the bar. She led him down the dark hall of private booths in back, sat him down, and waited for a new song to start.

"What's your background?" he asked her.

"Indian," she replied. He wanted to ask why this South Asian girl would be named for a desert in North Africa, but chose to let it go.

The song started. "You want extra?" she asked.

"What's extra?"

"Blow job."

"How much?"

"One hundred."

"Okay." She opened her purse. Michael Muhammad Knight was soft and little and didn't know if it would work, but she put the condom over his head and sucked, unrolling the rubber as he grew into it. Then she bobbed. The author swelled. Most of the erection was mental—he was getting head from a stripper! Then he looked up and noticed one of those tuxedoed bouncers standing behind the wall of their booth. They made eye contact for one second, then the bouncer turned and vanished into the darkness. How long had he been there? Was he going to rat out the author? What kind of laws did they have in Canada? Was he in some shit? Michael Muhammad Knight looked down at the stripper, who had no idea what he had just seen. Should he tell her? Were they both in trouble? Was someone going to slap her up and take what Michael Muhammad Knight had paid her? Could he bring himself to nut with all of this to worry about?

He could, and did, and she didn't even know, so he tapped her on the arm. She got up and told Michael Muhammad Knight to take off the condom. He peeled off the squishy latex and held it for a nervous, unsure second before she instructed him to drop it down the two-inch gap between the seat and the wall. The author released his spermy rubber into the crevice and wondered what else was back there. Then he reached into his pocket and handed her the hundred Canadian dollars. With the money in hand, she leaned over and kissed him on the cheek.

"Have a good night," she said. He thanked her and got up quickly, speed-walking back to his table. Amazing Ayyub was staring into his drink.

"Amazing Ayyub, we have to go!"

"Okay, Michael."

"Ayyub, get up! We really have to go. I'll explain in the car."

So the author stormed toward the door, Ayyub behind him. "Man," said Michael Muhammad Knight once they were outside, "I got head in there!" He turned around. Ayyub wasn't there. The author walked around the place— maybe Ayyub had sprinted to the car—but couldn't find him. He went back into the foyer, then past the men at the door, scanned the dark club, went back out to the parking lot, went back to his car. "AYYUB!" he barked. Michael Muhammad Knight feared the legal ramifications he faced, so he had to say, *Fuck it, I'm leaving Ayyub here*. He got in his Buick and drove down Lundy's Lane maybe a mile before turning back around. By then, Amazing Ayyub was waiting in front of the club. As soon as he got in the car, the author slapped him in the back of the head. "AYYUB, MAN, WE'RE IN SERIOUS SHIT RIGHT NOW! I JUST HAD A FUCKIN' HOOKER AND GOT CAUGHT!"

"I'M SORRY, MICHAEL!"

"YOU WERE RIGHT THERE BEHIND ME. WHERE'D YOU GO?" Michael Muhammad Knight had a hard time driving while still screaming at Amazing Ayyub. "WE WERE ABOUT TO GET SHOT UP AND LEFT IN A DITCH BY THESE SEX-INDUSTRY SCUMBAGS, AYYUB!"

"I'm sorry, Michael. I was getting a dance."

"A dance? You kept me waiting so you could get a dance?"

"I paid for your blow job, man. I just wanted a dance."

"We had some serious shit going on in there, Amazing Ayyub!"

"When we were walking out, I saw the hottest bitch ever and got a lap dance from her."

"Did you even understand our situation?"

"I just got one dance, bro, that's it. And I paid for your fucking head job."

"Ayyub, did you just say 'head job'?"

"Man, I gotta pee really bad."

"We're driving back to Buffalo, Amazing Ayyub."

"No, Michael! Lemme pee!"

"You crazy goddamned Twelver, you almost had us killed in there."

"MICHAEL, I NEED TO PEE! PULL OVER SOME-WHERE!"

"Okay, Ayyub, we'll go to Denny's and you're going to buy me a Grand Slam breakfast."

"MICHAEL, PLEEEEEEASE!"

"And you know, if they're checking everyone's trunks at the border, it'll be a long wait and you can just go and piss yourself."

"OKAY, MAN, I'LL BUY YOU A GRAND SLAM BREAKFAST!"

"Sounds fair."

They pulled into the parking lot, and Amazing Ayyub jumped out, running away as if the Skylark were on fire, before Michael Muhammad Knight could even stop the car. He swung open the Denny's doors and bolted for the men's room. Michael Muhammad Knight told the Denny's people that it was okay, the maniac was with him and just had to pee really bad. The author was seated at a booth and ordered the Grand Slam.

Amazing Ayyub emerged ten minutes later with a big smile on his face, looking even dumber for his wrinkled button-up shirt.

"I feel better now, Michael. And I just saved money, too."

"What do you mean?"

"Man, I paid for your head job. But I just nutted for free, or at least for the price of a Grand Slam."

"DAMMIT! Amazing Ayyub, d'you beat off in there?"

"It's in the Q, bro. You can pound what your right hand

possesses—that's what it says."

"With all due respect, Amazing Ayyub, I appreciate you buying me head and a Grand Slam—"

"You're my friend, man. You let me stay on your couch."

"But yeah, anyway, with all due respect, you're still a fuckin' scumbag."

"I mooch off you for a place to stay," Ayyub countered. "You mooch off me for whores." Ayyub had him there. Halfway through the Grand Slam, Michael Muhammad Knight realized that he was eating bacon, and remembered how a couple of desi ex-girlfriends had declared it off-limits for him. The way he felt, the sad author would rather have had the girls.

"So this is our last night," he said. "What now?"

"Tomorrow's the Time," Ayyub answered. "By the Time, verily man is fucked."

"Are you sure you're ready?"

"The Time comes when it comes."

Back in the living room on Herman Street, Michael Muhammad Knight sat on a lawn chair while Amazing Ayyub threw himself into the couch, still wearing his wrinkled button-up. "The last night, bro," said the Amazing One. "Here it is."

"Amazing Ayyub, did I ever tell you about Omar X?" Ayyub shook his head, so Michael Muhammad Knight told the story: Omar X was the Thai-desi singer for the hardcore band Rogue Nation. After the tsunami, Omar had gone to South Thailand to hang with Muslim separatists. He'd written the author to tell him that the rebels weren't fundamentalist Al-Qaeda maniacs, they were good people with reasonable ideas. If anything, it reminded him of the situation in Quebec. Omar X had also said that he'd ventured to Phi Phi Island right after the tsunami and heard stories of how in Banda Aceh, the only things left standing were mosques. The Muslim island of Koh Lay was completely unharmed, but the neighboring tourist trap of Koh Mak ("where foreigners go to drink and fuck") was wiped out. Then, on Koh Lanta, the bars and beach bungalows were destroyed, while the Muslims weren't hit at all. "Sure makes you believe in God," Omar X had told Michael Muhammad Knight, who told Amazing Ayyub. "Crazy shit."

"That *is* crazy shit," said Ayyub. "That's heavy, bro." Ayyub took out his Ya Sin and read without making niyya to turn invisible—he read it just to read it. The Prophet had said that whoever read one letter of the Qur'an would receive a hasanah for it, and every hasanah would be multiplied by ten, and on top of that, Ya Sin was a special sura, the Heart of the Qur'an. Imam Al-Qurtubi reported in his Tafsir that Ibn 'Abbas narrated the Prophet as saying that to recite Ya Sin at the beginning of the day makes the rest of your day easy until the night comes, and reading it at nightfall would give you ease until sunrise. Al-Tirmidhi reported the Prophet as having said that someone who reads Ya Sin for Allah's sake will have his sins forgiven. Amazing Ayyub had a hard time with some of the words, and sometimes he sounded pathetic. Michael Muhammad Knight listened quietly until the end.

They'd drive to the Yazid TV studio in broad daylight, Amazing Ayyub's ultimate weapon filling the back seat and hanging out of the trunk. The gun wouldn't even have fit, had Ayyub not taken off the banana clip. With the Kominas in the tape deck, Ayyub remembered Basim and the martyred Shahjehan in Al Rukn's zombie-hunter training film. "Did you see my gun?" he asked the author.

"Of course I saw your gun, Amazing Ayyub; it's goddamned huge and takes up the whole car."

"It's like a Zulfikar, right? That's what I call it—Zulfikar." Ayyub pulled off Yusuf Islam's dad's Brooks Brothers shirt and threw it to the back seat, then looked down at his chest as though reading the weathered ink.

The author pulled onto the 290, where Ayyub spotted a green-laced Doc Marten on the shoulder of the road. Made him quiet for a moment. "Yo," he said finally, "remember when we showed up at Channel 7 on Elmwood at, like, two in the morning and I pounded on the door? I screamed at the janitor, all 'PUT ME ON TV OR I'LL BREAK YOUR JAW!'"

"That was a great time, Ayyub."

"That's what I should do today. And remember when we were driving up and down Chippewa, yelling at all the club sluts?"

"I remember that time you had the fishing pole and you were sticking it out of the car at them."

"And I was like, 'C'MERE AND TOUCH MY POLE!' C'mere and touch the spiritual pole of the time, ha-ha. It's not so bad being Ayyub."

Michael Muhammad Knight took exit 5B and in a matter of minutes was turning into the parking lot. "I wonder which one they came in," said Ayyub, squinting at the parked cars, looking for anything special that'd connect one to his intended victims. Once Michael Muhammad Knight found a space and stopped the car, Ayyub jumped out like an excited boy at the toy store. "You want to look for cans and bottles?"

"Sure," the author shrugged. So they tramped around the station's surrounding asphalt desert. Amazing Ayyub had a good eye for cans and bottles that were far away; he'd zero in and make a beeline, as though in competition with other recycling predators out there. "LOOK AT ME!" he screamed, "I HAVE AN EMPTY CAN!" He darted across the parking lot after two full bottles of Vanilla Coke. "That's a dime right there." Ayyub twisted off the caps, held the bottles at his crotch, and emptied them like a double-barreled penis. The Coke fizzed on the ground. "Who'd want to drink this nonsense?" he asked. "Look at that—it'll peel paint off a car, but people want to put it in their bodies?" Then Ayyub spotted a discarded Marlboro box and picked it up to get the Marlboro Miles. Each pack was good for five Marlboro Miles, he told Michael Muhammad Knight. You get five hundred Marlboro Miles, and Marlboro will give you a nice jacket or comparable merchandise bearing the Marlboro logo. Ayyub retrieved an empty Timberland bag for his bottles and cans. The author came across a bottle, but Ayyub said not to take that one, that was piss in there. "Somebody must have slept in his car here last night," Ayyub observed. "Fuck it, bro, we don't need somebody's piss bottle. We've got sixty tax-free cents, and we didn't have to take any orders. NO MINUTE RICE FOR ME TONIGHT— I'M GOIN' TO RED LOBSTER!"

Ayyub walked tough. "I'm a nervy fuck," he told Michael Muhammad Knight. Damn straight. Ayyub put their bag of bottles and cans in the author's car and pulled out Basim's big machine gun, the new Zulfikar. For a while they stood by Michael Muhammad Knight's car, Amazing Ayyub with the gun resting on his shoulder. "We're the good guys," asked Ayyub, gaze lowered. "Right, bro?"

"Why wouldn't we be?" replied the author.

"Maybe the Shah 79 guys are okay for their own thing, you know what I mean?"

"No, Ayyub. I don't."

"Fuck, man, I don't know what I'm saying. It's hard to say it."

"It's not about good guys and bad guys; there's always going to be Shah 79, and there's always going to be Amazing Ayyub. Just play the part that you've been assigned and do your duty."

"That's what it's all about."

"Al-Kharraz said that we know Allah by His bringing together of opposites, you know, so we . . . aw, fuck it, Ayyub. Shah 79 sucks. They're ruining everything."

"Did you know that the Fifth and Sixth Imams both opposed armed rebellion?"

"I always saw you more as Number Three, Ayyub. Karbala's on your heart."

"That's right, brother."

"You know what 'Ayyub' means?"

"Isn't it . . . uh, no, what's it mean?"

"It means Job."

"Yeah, yeah, that's what I thought it meant."

"You know who Job was, Amazing Job?"

"He was that guy."

"He soaked up some heavy shit from the world, man. Allah hit him with crazy trouble."

"And Jesus told him to wait, right?"

"Something like that. You ever hear of Mad Mehmet?"

"Wasn't that the taqwacore version of GG Allin, the guy who used to smear poop on himself and run around—"

"No, Ayyub. Mad Mehmet was a medieval shaykh in the Malamatiyyas. He used to smoke dope and get drunk and ride on Rumi's tomb."

"So, he was taqwacore?"

"I'm not sure about that. But I could see you guys hanging out, at least." Michael Muhammad Knight then sang the opening lines to an old Rancid song, inserting new names: *Mehmet and Ayyub, two friends of mine/skinheads what they claim/outside similarities but they don't feel the same/Ayyub thinks Mehmet's a mod, and Mehmet thinks Ayyub's a punk/ Mehmet listens to ska and Ayyub likes Last Resort . . .*

Michael Muhammad Knight then looked at Amazing Ayyub and immediately, clearly, understood him to be the last lonely survivor of an extinct race. Made the author want to tell him to quit settling for hand jobs—for the future's sake, Ayyub, throw it *in* a few times!

"Where are you going?" asked Michael Muhammad Knight. "I mean, after?"

"First off, I've still got this," replied the gunman, whipping out the Ya Sin that Basim had given him in the desert, "so no one's gonna see me. I can bust out of the studio and head up the stairwell to the roof and just get out of here. Shit, I could even hop in the elevator if I wanted to—I'll be invisible."

"So you're going to the roof, and then what?"

"I'm flying to Brockport, brother. Insha'Allah, fuck it."

Amazing Ayyub made his niyya, read Ya Sin, and vanished. Beyond its function as an invisiblity spell, Ya Sin doubled as a prayer for the dead and dying. "My dad came over here for school," said a voice out of thin air.

"Is that right, Ayyub?"

"Yeah, bro. He got a PhD in muff diving."

Listening to invisible Ayyub's footsteps as he went off on his death march, Michael Muhammad Knight wondered if Ayyub knew another sura that gave him the power of flight.

The author then turned away, looking past the far end of the parking lot and across the street to a woman in full black niqab, black abaya, black gloves, black boots (the girl's a time bomb). She waited for a pause in traffic, calmly crossed, and then bolted toward him at a full sprint, robes flowing behind her, looking like a soldier from some other, feudal time. Michael Muhammad Knight had ample time to register that she was running to him with violence in mind, but he just stayed and watched, staring at her long enough for his brain to break her down into an abstract, disjointed thing, the cloak no longer fluid and flowing but flat and geometric and segmented like the armor of a samurai. He perceived it as a cluster of metal sheets spray-painted black and fastened to her body with ten thousand rivets penetrating her skin everywhere—she had become a sex mutant to him. The abaya was an exoskeleton building her up from the outside, and her cavities remained guarded with invincible titanium steel. Her sword, oversize like Ayyub's gun, was also bolted into her hand to become an extension of her body, an elongated slicing arm. The curve of her blade was nearly drastic enough to resemble a sharp crescent. Beneath the steel wrapped around her head was a core of bone to house the computer, no longer a suffering brain, now more machine Robo-Rabeya than Islamic feminist— like an Islamic feminist Darth Vader.

She was soon close enough that Michael Muhammad Knight could hear her feet hitting the pavement. It seemed as though she could run for ten thousand years across the fields of his trance life and never get to him, but she did, close enough to become organic again, her niqab and abaya returning to soft fabrics with creases and folds, and trailing behind her like a billowing black flag covered in band patches—and then she was close enough for him to see the slit for her eyes and realize that the person inside the cloak wanted to kill him. The old wrestling play-by-play announcers used to remark on the psychological advantages a wrestler in a mask had: No one could read his face to know if he was hurt or mad, confident or scared. Michael Muhammad Knight couldn't read Rabeya's eyes until she was on her way to do it. She performed a kind of hop and in midair brought her right foot behind her; then, in the second when her left foot planted on the ground, it pushed off and her right sailed upward toward Michael Muhammad Knight's chin. The author fell backward onto the hood of his car, then rolled off onto the ground.

By the time Michael Muhammad Knight could even comprehend the pain and know what had happened, Rabeya was standing over him, holding her Zulfikar.

"FUCK YOU!" she screamed with a swift combat boot to his ribs. "ALL YOU WHITE CONVERT BOYS THINK YOU'RE FUCKING INDIANA JONES! FUCK YOU!" She kicked him again.

"Rabeya—"

"You all think you're going somewhere that no Caucasian has ever been able to go . . ."

"That's not true, there's the Bosni—"

"Don't say the Bosnians! Don't try to feel less weird about yourself by bringing up the white Muslims in Bosnia, when all you really want Islam to do is make you less white! Look back on yourself at fifteen, so proud that you could pray in another language and take on strange new names that set you apart from everyone in your white world. You flash your Malcolm X autobiographies; you want to touch his big blackness. You love the war on terror and you get off on your middle name scaring the soccer moms in Minnesota. But it's never real for you, Mike—it's post-9/11 fantasy camp, a kufi you can take off, a beard you can shave. You don't have to deal with it when you don't want to. And then you get so fucking righteous. You're a revert, right, since you were born in a natural state of Islam and now you've *reverted* to your true self?"

"You don't know where I'm coming from."

"No, Mike, I know you've got a dad up in the Shenandoah sticks with his Hitler books telling you that if you have sex with a white girl on a freshly covered grave, she turns black. You have as much cultural baggage as any of us. And now you hang out with the Five Percenters. What do they call you?"

"Azreal Wisdom."

"Well, *I* call you Indiana Jones," she snapped, stepping back to catch her breath, still holding the sword. "You think you can just swagger into the brown man's temple and sneak out with his idol."

"I'm Muslim," said the author, manipulating his face into a smirk. "There's no idol in the mosque."

"Bullshit!" She kicked him again. "Like you don't know. Like you haven't watched us guard it with our lives, building up these masjids only as traps to keep it from ever escaping.

Of course we have an idol, and it's more precious than the Prophet; it's treasured even more than Allah's Qur'an."

"What is?"

"PUSSY! Mike, it's all about pussy. Islam's idol is an unbroken vagina." The occasional cracks and trembles in her voice led Michael Muhammad Knight to wonder if his *niqabi* riot grrl was crying. "If Indiana Jones wants to steal the heart of Islam," she continued, "he has to get behind those dividers in the masjid, climb up the balcony or go down to the basement, find the women's section, wherever they put it, and fuck all the brown girls. To the uncles you're a trophy, but you still watch us through a hole in the wall. You know that you're not in, not really, not fully, until you get yourself a shaved houri and ritually tear her open."

"I'm sorry, Rabeya."

"Michael Muhammad Knight, in the end you're just another phallocentric orientalist, and I'm putting an end to your bullshit sand-wigger discourse right now."

"What's going to happen?" asked the sand-wigger author, though he already knew.

"It's not a blow job at the punk show," Rabeya answered, now holding her sword with a double grip. Time for the Awesome Correction . . .

Then came a muffled rattle of heavy machine-gun fire coming from inside the studio.

"What was that?" Rabeya asked.

"Amazing Ayyub assassinating a Muslim emo band."

Ayyub had so many problems, and there was no reason at

all for him to make it in life, but at least he could pull this off. Shah 79 was dead, and the taqwacore scene had been saved. The author knew his own role: He closed his eyes and lowered his head to offer her a clean shot to his neck. Rabeya looked at the author and saw that this was also the time to realize her own holy purpose, so she swung her sword.

Upon the second and third blows, the author's head was severed entirely and fell to the pavement. Rabeya took off running, in what direction, the author had no idea. He was still alive, with enough blood in his head to keep his brain going for another fifteen to twenty seconds, or even half a minute or more. Michael Muhammad Knight wondered whether there'd be a next step in his purification: perhaps two of Allah's angels cutting open his scrotum and scooping out his testes to perform a ritual washing, then gently putting them back—except he no longer had a scrotum, or testes or arms or legs or a spinal cord.

Michael Muhammad Knight opened his eyes. He couldn't see the rest of him slumped over maybe four or five feet away, but he could look up and out of the corner of his eye glimpse what appeared to be a giant, flat paper bird soaring from the roof. It wasn't a paper bird—it was a hang glider that looked to have no pilot, just flying with a mind and power of its own, but Michael Muhammad Knight knew what Ya Sin could do for a mushashin.

Brockport, a suburb of Rochester, was maybe fifty miles away. Michael Muhammad Knight couldn't know what it offered; maybe the state college there hosted a small clique of displaced taqwacores ready to worship Amazing Ayyub as their shaykh and name him Hamza Yusuf of the fuck-ups, king of the Zaytuna rejects, selling lectures that were only microtape recordings of hand jobs at the homeless shelter.

AFTERWORD

It took four years for this book to come out. I first wrote the story in 2005, and sold it to the UK publisher of my first novel. However, after heavily censoring *The Taqwacores*, and learning that censored versions of novels don't sell, they dropped me and cancelled their release of *Osama Van Halen*. Thank Allah for Soft Skull Press, which has re-released both *The Taqwacores* and now *Osama Van Halen* fully intact.

At the time that I wrote *Osama Van Halen,* many American Muslims were excited by the prospects of Bridges TV, a new cable channel created specifically for our community. I had met its founder, Muzammil Hassan, at his booth during the 2005 convention of the Islamic Society of North America (ISNA). I asked him if he was looking for writers, and he said that he'd love to see what I had. We shared a good conversation, but I never sent him anything; while Bridges TV seemed like a positive thing for Muslims, I couldn't imagine it hiring a Muslim like me.

It just so happened that Bridges TV was headquartered in Buffalo, my home for several years and the setting for *The Taqwacores*. When I imagined Amazing Ayyub on a mission to rescue Islamic punk rock from emo, it made sense for Buffalo to host the final battle—with Ayyub assassinating emo kids at the studios of a Muslim cable channel. It also seemed right to insert myself into the story as a fictional character, miserable with Amazing Ayyub in a squalid house on Herman Street, where I had lived while writing *The Taqwacores*.

The coincidences have now gone from absurd to horrific. The ending of the novel, in which Rabeya decapitates me in the studio's parking lot, would become a perverse mirror of real-life tragedy: on February 13, 2009, Muzammil Hassan was arrested for allegedly beheading his wife, Aasiya, in the offices of Bridges TV.

My initial reaction to the news was the same as everyone's. It's always hard to confront these things, these proofs of how terrible human beings can be; to consider the mind of the killer, the special brutality of the crime, and the suffering of an innocent person in her last moments and the loved ones that are left behind. After a week of conversations that started with "Oh my god, did you hear what happened in Buffalo?" I was discussing the murder with a journalist friend and finally recognized what was in my novel—which had just been submitted for the galleys and a summer release.

I wrote about a fictional woman who swung her sword and took heads as feminist justice. She did her deed at a fictional Islamic TV station in a fictional Buffalo; but at the corresponding spot in the real Buffalo, patriarchy destroyed a real person in the same fashion. The connection is a freakish, unbelievable accident that I never could have foreseen. All I can say is that I wrote this story four years earlier, and I'm sorry.

While we're on it, I'm proud of the Muslim community's response; particularly the statement by Imam Mohamed Hagmagid Ali, vice president of ISNA. "I call upon my fellow imams and community leaders," he said, "to never second-guess a woman who comes to us indicating that she feels her life to be in danger." The survivor of abuse who seeks divorce, he added, "should not be viewed as someone who has brought shame to herself or her family. The shame is on the person who committed the act of violence or abuse."

The Hassan tragedy sparked honest and heartfelt discussion throughout the Muslim blogs. Some writers were overly apologetic on our religion's behalf, claiming that domestic violence has no basis in Islam. That's not exactly true; we still must take a hard look at verse 4:34, as well as shari'a conceptions of marriage that allow for spousal rape; but it is true, as the imam reminds us, that the Prophet never abused his wives. Maybe Islam's best part can correct its worst.

The first non-Muslim statement I read came from the National Organization for Women (NOW), which called the murder "terroristic" and an "honor killing." Months earlier, a young Muslim woman murdered in Toronto was given similar treatment, understood only as a victim of Islam. Some used the incident as proof that multiculturalism would destroy Canada. *This is what brown men do to brown women*, we are told—since in the white world, violence of men upon women is obviously an aberration from the norm, with no special term to explain it.

Neglecting to use my middle name in an email to NOW, I wrote only as Michael Knight, a white man from a white family. I told them that my white Christian mother was terrorized physically and psychologically by a white Christian man who slept with the Bible under his shirt. My mother was beaten, raped, held hostage, and threatened with a knife to her baby's throat. If my father buried us in the mountains, as he had promised repeatedly to do, would anyone call it an "honor killing"?

Women in that kind of house either get out or die. When I was two years old, my mother got us out. Over ten years later, I was reunited with my father. The first day I met him, he told me, "Woman is the nigger of the world." Not the Muslim world, or the white man's world. The world. Salam to Aasiya Hassan, Aqsa Parvez, Nancy Benoit, and Daniel Benoit, all the ones who can't get out, all the women and children left to Allah's care alone, may he surround them with care.

Michael Muhammad Knight
February 20, 2009

ACKNOWLEDGMENTS

PEACE

Richard Nash, Anne Horowitz, Adam Krefman, Annie Tucker, and everyone at Soft Skull Press.

Sonia Pabley and Phyllis Wender at the Gersh Agency.

SALAM

Laury Silvers, for swinging the sharpest sword, and sharpening mine.